W.W. JACOBS – THE SHORT STORIES
VOLUME 3

William Wymark Jacobs was born on September 8th, 1863 in the Wapping district of London, England. Jacobs grew up near the docks, where his father was a wharf manager. The docks and river side would be a constant theme of his writing in years to come.

Although surrounded by poverty, he received a formal education in London, first at a private prep school and later at the Birkbeck Literary and Scientific Institute.

His working life began with a less than exciting clerical position at the Post Office Savings Bank. Jacobs put his imagination to good use writing short stories, sketches and articles, many for the Post Office house publication "Blackfriars Magazine."

In 1896 Jacobs published Many Cargoes, a selection of sea-faring yarns, which established him as a popular writer with a knack for authentic dialogue and trick endings.

A year later he published a novelette, The Skipper's Wooing, and in 1898 another collection of short stories; Sea Urchins. These works painted vivid pictures of dockland and seafaring London full of colourful characters.

By 1899, Jacobs was able to quit the post office and write full-time.

He married the noted suffragist Agnes Eleanor Williams (who had been jailed for her protest activities) in 1900. They set up households both in Loughton, Essex and in central London.

The publication in 1902 of At Sunwich Port and Dialstone Lane, in 1904, cemented Jacobs' reputation as one of the leading British authors of the new century.

There followed a string of further successful publications, including Captain's All (1905), Night Watches (1914), The Castaways (1916), and Sea Whispers (1926).

Though Jacobs would create little in the way of new work after 1911, he still wrote and was recognized as a leading humorist, ranked alongside such writers as P. G. Wodehouse.

William Wymark Jacobs died in a North London nursing home in Hornsey Lane, Islington on September 1st, 1943.

Index of Contents

BEDRIDDEN

July 12, 1915.—Disquieting rumours to the effect that epidemic of Billetitis hitherto confined to the north of King's Road shows signs of spreading.

July 14.—Report that two Inns of Court men have been seen peeping over my gate.

July 16.—Informed that soldier of agreeable appearance and charming manners requests interview with me. Took a dose of Phospherine and went. Found composite photograph of French, Joffre, and Hindenburg waiting for me in the hall. Smiled (he did, I mean) and gave me the mutilated form of salute reserved for civilians. Introduced himself as Quartermaster-Sergeant Beddem, and stated that the Inns of Court O.T.C. was going under canvas next week. After which he gulped. Meantime could I take in a billet. Questioned as to what day the corps was going into camp said that he believed it was Monday, but was not quite sure—might possibly be Tuesday. Swallowed again and coughed a little. Accepted billet and felt completely re-warded by smile. Q.M.S. bade me good-bye, and then with the air of a man suddenly remembering something, asked me whether I could take two. Excused myself and interviewed my C.O. behind the dining-room door. Came back and accepted. Q.M.S. so overjoyed (apparently) that he fell over the scraper. Seemed to jog his memory. He paused, and gazing in absent fashion at the topmost rose on the climber in the porch, asked whether I could take three! Added hopefully that the third was only a boy. Excused myself. Heated debate with C.O. Subject: sheets. Returned with me to explain to the Q.M.S. He smiled. C.O. accepted at once, and, returning smile, expressed regret at size and position of bedrooms available. Q.M.S. went off swinging cane jauntily.

July 17.—Billets arrived. Spoke to them about next Monday and canvas. They seemed surprised. Strange how the military authorities decline to take men into their confidence merely because they are privates. Let them upstairs. They went (for first and last time) on tiptoe.

July 18.—Saw Q.M.S. Beddem in the town. Took shelter in the King's Arms.

Jug. 3.—Went to Cornwall.

Aug. 31.—Returned. Billets received me very hospitably.

Sept. 4.—Private Budd, electrical engineer, dissatisfied with appearance of bell-push in dining-room, altered it.

Sept. 5.—Bells out of order.

Sept. 6.—Private Merited, also an electrical engineer, helped Private Budd to repair bells.

Sept. 7.—Private Budd helped Private Merited to repair bells.

Sept. 8.—Privates Budd and Merited helped each other to repair bells.

Sept. 9.—Sent to local tradesman to put my bells in order.

Sept. 15.—Told that Q.M.S. Beddem wished to see me. Saw C.O. first. She thought he had possibly come to take some of the billets away. Q.M.S. met my approach with a smile that re-minded me vaguely of picture-postcards I had seen. Awfully sorry to trouble me, but Private Montease, just back from three weeks' holiday with bronchitis, was sleeping in the wood-shed on three planks and a tin-tack. Beamed at me and waited. Went and bought another bed-stead.

Sept. 16.—Private Montease and a cough entered into residence.

Sept. 17, 11.45 p.m.—Maid came to bedroom-door with some cough lozenges which she asked me to take to the new billet. Took them. Private Montease thanked me, but said he didn't mind coughing. Said it was an heirloom; Montease cough, known in highest circles all over Scotland since time of Young Pretender.

Sept. 20.—Private Montease installed in easy-chair in dining-room with touch of bronchitis, looking up trains to Bournemouth.

Sept. 21.—Private Montease in bed all day. Cook anxious "to do her bit" rubbed his chest with home-made embrocation. Believe it is same stuff she rubs chests in hall with. Smells the same anyway.

Sept. 24.—Private Montease, complaining of slight rawness of chest, but otherwise well, returned to duty.

Oct. 5.—Cough worse again. Private Montease thinks that with care it may turn to bronchitis. Borrowed an A.B.C.

Oct. 6.—Private Montease relates uncanny experience. Woke up with feeling of suffocation to find an enormous black-currant and glycerine jujube wedged in his gullet. Never owned such a thing in his life. Seems to be unaware that he always sleeps with his mouth open.

Nov. 14.—Private Bowser, youngest and tallest of my billets, gazetted.

Nov. 15, 10.35 a.m.—Private Bowser in tip-top spirits said good-bye to us all.

10.45.—Told that Q.M.S. Beddem desired to see me. Capitulated. New billet, Private Early, armed to the teeth, turned up in the evening. Said that he was a Yorkshireman. Said that Yorkshire was the finest county in England, and Yorkshiremen the finest men in the world. Stood toying with his bayonet and waiting for contradiction.

Jan. 5, 1916.—Standing in the garden just after lunch was witness to startling phenomenon. Q.M.S. Beddem came towards front-gate with a smile so expansive that gate after first trembling violently on its hinges swung open of its own accord. Q.M.S., with smile (sad), said he was in trouble. Very old member of the Inns of Court, Private Keen, had re-joined, and he wanted a good billet for him. Would cheerfully give up his own bed, but it wasn't long enough. Not to be outdone in hospitality by my own gate accepted Private Keen. Q.M.S. digging hole in my path with toe of right boot, and for first and only time manifesting signs of nervousness, murmured that two life-long friends of Private Keen's had rejoined with him. Known as the Three Inseparables. Where they were to sleep, unless I—. Fled to house, and locking myself in top-attic watched Q.M.S. from window. He departed with bent head and swagger-cane reversed.

Jan 6.—Private Keen arrived. Turned out to be son of an old Chief of mine. Resolved not to visit the sins of the father on the head of a child six feet two high and broad in proportion.

Feb. 6.—Private Keen came home with a temperature.

Feb. 7.—M.O. diagnosed influenza. Was afraid it would spread.

Feb. 8.—Warned the other four billets. They seemed amused. Pointed out that influenza had no terrors for men in No. 2 Company, who were doomed to weekly night-ops. under Major Carryon.

Feb. 9.—House strangely and pleasantly quiet. Went to see how Private Keen was progressing, and found the other four billets sitting in a row on his bed practising deep-breathing exercises.

Feb. 16.—Billets on night-ops. until late hour. Spoke in highest terms of Major Carryon's marching powers—also in other terms.

March 3.—Waited up until midnight for Private Merited, who had gone to Slough on his motor-bike.

March 4, 1.5 a.m.—Awakened by series of explosions from over-worked, or badly-worked, motor-bike. Put head out of window and threw key to Private Merited. He seemed excited. Said he had been chased all the way from Chesham by a pink rat with yellow spots. Advised him to go to bed. Set him an example.

1.10. a.m.—Heard somebody in the pantry. 2.10. a.m.—Heard Private Merited going upstairs to bed.

2.16 a.m.—Heard Private Merited still going upstairs to bed.

2.20-3.15. a.m.—Heard Private Merited getting to bed.

April 3, 12.30 a.m.—Town-hooter announced Zeppelins and excited soldier called up my billets from their beds to go and frighten them off. Pleasant to see superiority of billets over the hooter: that only emitted three blasts.

12.50 a.m.—Billets returned with exception of Private Merited, who was retained for sake of his motor-bike.

9 a.m.—On way to bath-room ran into Private Merited, who, looking very glum and sleepy, inquired whether I had a copy of the Exchange and Mart in the house.

10 p.m.—Overheard billets discussing whether it was worth while removing boots before going to bed until the Zeppelin scare was over. Joined in discussion.

May 2.—Rumours that the Inns of Court were going under canvas. Discredited them.

May 5.—Rumours grow stronger.

May 6.—Billets depressed. Begin to think perhaps there is something in rumours after all.

May 9.-All doubts removed. Tents begin to spring up with the suddenness of mushrooms in fields below Berkhamsted Place.

May 18, LIBERATION DAY.—Bade a facetious good-bye to my billets; response lacking in bonhomie.

May 19.-House delightfully quiet. Presented caller of unkempt appearance at back-door with remains of pair of military boots, three empty shaving-stick tins, and a couple of partially bald tooth-brushes.

May 21.—In afternoon went round and looked at camp. Came home smiling, and went to favourite seat in garden to smoke. Discovered Private Early lying on it fast asleep. Went to study. Private Merited at table writing long and well-reasoned letter to his tailor. As he said he could never write properly with anybody else in the room, left him and went to bath-room. Door locked. Peevish but familiar voice, with a Scotch accent, asked me what I wanted; also complained of temperature of water.

May 22.—After comparing notes with neighbours, feel deeply grateful to Q.M.S. Beddem for sending me the best six men in the corps.

July 15.—Feel glad to have been associated, however remotely and humbly, with a corps, the names of whose members appear on the Roll of Honour of every British regiment.

THE WINTER OFFENSIVE

N.B.—Having regard to the eccentricities of the Law of Libel it must be distinctly understood that the following does not refer to the distinguished officer, Lieut. Troup Horne, of the Inns of Court. Anybody trying to cause mischief between a civilian of eight stone and a soldier of seventeen by a statement to the contrary will hear from my solicitors.

Aug. 29, 1916.—We returned from the sea to find our house still our own, and the military still in undisputed possession of the remains of the grass in the fields of Berkhamsted Place. As in previous years, it was impossible to go in search of wild-flowers without stumbling over sleeping members of the Inns of Court; but war is war, and we grumble as little as possible.

Sept. 28.—Unpleasant rumours to the effect that several members of the Inns of Court had attributed cases of curvature of the spine to sleeping on ground that had been insufficiently rolled. Also that they had been heard to smack their lips and speak darkly of featherbeds. Respected neighbour of gloomy disposition said that if Pharaoh were still alive he could suggest an eleventh plague to him beside which frogs and flies were an afternoon's diversion.

Oct. 3.—Householders of Berkhamsted busy mending bedsteads broken by last year's billets, and buying patent taps for their beer-barrels.

Oct. 15.—Informed that a representative of the Army wished to see me. Instead of my old friend Q.M.S. Beddem, who generally returns to life at this time of year, found that it was an officer of magnificent presence and two pips. A fine figure of a man, with a great resemblance to the late lamented Bismarck, minus the moustache and the three hairs on the top of the head. Asked him to be seated. He selected a chair that was all arms and legs and no hips to speak of and crushed himself into it. After which he unfastened his belt and "swelled wisibly afore my werry eyes." Said that his name was True Born and asked if it made any difference to me whether I had one officer or half-a-dozen men billeted on me. Said that he was the officer, and that as the rank-and-file were not allowed to pollute the same atmosphere, thought I should score. After a mental review of all I could remember of the Weights and Measures Table, accepted him. He bade a lingering farewell to the chair, and departed.

Oct. 16.—Saw Q.M.S. Beddem on the other side of the road and gave him an absolutely new thrill by crossing to meet him. Asked diffidently—as diffidently as he could, that is—how many men my house would hold. Replied eight—or ten at a pinch. He gave me a surprised and beaming smile and whipped out a huge note-book. Informed him with as much regret as I could put into a voice not always under perfect control, that I had already got an officer. Q.M.S., favouring me with a look very appropriate to the Devil's Own, turned on his heel and set off in pursuit of a lady-billetee, pulling up short on the threshold of the baby-linen shop in which she took refuge. Left him on guard with a Casablanca-like look on his face.

Nov. 1.—Lieut. True Born took up his quarters with us. Gave him my dressing-room for bedchamber. Was awakened several times in the night by what I took to be Zeppelins, flying low.

Nov. 2.—Lieut. True Born offered to bet me five pounds to twenty that the war would be over by 1922.

Nov. 3.—Offered to teach me auction-bridge.

Nov. 4.—Asked me whether I could play "shove ha'penny."

Nov. 10.—Lieut. True Born gave one of the regimental horses a riding-lesson. Came home grumpy and went to bed early.

Nov. 13.—Another riding-lesson. Over-heard him asking one of the maids whether there was such a thing as a water-bed in the house.

Nov. 17.—Complained bitterly of horse-copers. Said that his poor mount was discovered to be suffering from saddle-soreness, broken wind, splints, weak hocks, and two bones of the neck out of place.

Dec. 9.—7 p.m.—One of last year's billets, Private Merited, on leave from a gunnery course, called to see me and to find out whether his old bed had improved since last year. Left his motor-bike in the garage, and the smell in front of the dining-room window.

8 to 12 p.m.—Sat with Private Merited, listening to Lieut. True Born on the mistakes of Wellington.

12.5 a.m.—Rose to go to bed. Was about to turn out gas in hall when I discovered the lieutenant standing with his face to the wall playing pat-a-cake with it. Gave him three-parts of a tumbler of brandy. Said he felt better and went upstairs. Arrived in his bed-room, he looked about him carefully, and then, with a superb sweep of his left arm, swept the best Chippendale looking-glass in the family off the dressing table and dived face down-wards to the floor, missing death and the corner of the chest of drawers by an inch.

12:15 a.m.—Rolled him on to his back and got his feet on the bed. They fell off again as soon as they were cleaner than the quilt. The lieutenant, startled by the crash, opened his eyes and climbed into bed unaided.

12.20 a.m.—Sent Private Merited for the M.O., Captain Geranium.

12.25 a.m.—Mixed a dose of brandy and castor-oil in a tumbler. Am told it slips down like an oyster that way—bad oyster, I should think. Lieut. True Born jibbed. Reminded him that England expects that every man will take his castor-oil. Reply unprintable. Apologized a moment later. Said that his mind was wandering and that he thought he was a colonel. Reassured him.

12.40 a.m.—Private Merited returned with the M.O. Latter nicely dressed in musical-comedy pyjamas of ravishing hue, and great-coat, with rose-tinted feet thrust into red morocco slippers. Held consultation and explained my treatment. M.O. much impressed, anxious to know whether I was a doctor. Told him "No," but that I knew all the ropes. First give patient castor-oil, then diet him and call every day to make sure that he doesn't like his food. After that, if he shows signs of getting well too soon, give him a tonic. . . . M.O. stuffy.

Dec. 10.—M.O. diagnosed attack as due to something which True Born believes to be tobacco, with which he disinfects the house, the mess-sheds, and the streets of Berkhamsted.

Dec. 11.—True Born, shorn of thirteen pipes a day out of sixteen, disparages the whole race of M.O.'s.

Dec. 14.—He obtains leave to attend wedding of a great-aunt and ransacks London for a specialist who advocates strong tobacco.

Dec. 15.—He classes specialists with M.O.'s. Is surprised (and apparently disappointed) that, so far, the breaking of the looking-glass has brought me no ill-luck. Feel somewhat uneasy myself until glass is repaired by local cabinet-maker.

Jan. 10, 1917.—Lieut. True Born starts to break in another horse.

Feb. 1.—Horse broken.

March 3.—Running short of tobacco, go to my billet's room and try a pipe of his. Take all the remedies except the castor-oil.

April 4, 8.30 a.m.—Awakened by an infernal crash and discover that my poor looking-glass is in pieces again on the floor. True Born explains that its position, between the open door and the open window, was too much for it. Don't believe a word of it. Shall believe to my dying day that it burst in a frantic but hopeless attempt to tell Lieut. True Born the truth, the whole truth, and nothing but the truth.

April 6.—The lieutenant watching for some sign of misfortune to me. Says that I can't break a mirror twice without ill-luck following it. Me!

April 9.—Lieut. True Born comes up to me with a face full of conflicting emotions. "Your ill-luck has come at last," he says with gloomy satisfaction. "We go under canvas on the 23rd. You are losing me!"

THE BEQUEST

R. Robert Clarkson sat by his fire, smoking thoughtfully. His lifelong neighbour and successful rival in love had passed away a few days before, and Mr. Clarkson, fresh from the obsequies, sat musing on the fragility of man and the inconvenience that sometimes attended his departure.

His meditations were disturbed by a low knocking on the front door, which opened on to the street. In response to his invitation it opened slowly, and a small middle-aged man of doleful aspect entered softly and closed it behind him.

"Evening, Bob," he said, in stricken accents. "I thought I'd just step round to see how you was bearing up. Fancy pore old Phipps! Why, I'd a'most as soon it had been me. A'most."

Mr. Clarkson nodded.

"Here to-day and gone to-morrow," continued Mr. Smithson, taking a seat. "Well, well! So you'll have her at last-pore thing."

"That was his wish," said Mr. Clarkson, in a dull voice.

"And very generous of him too," said Mr. Smithson. "Everybody is saying so. Certainly he couldn't take her away with him. How long is it since you was both of you courting her?"

"Thirty years come June," replied the other.

"Shows what waiting does, and patience," commented Mr. Smithson. "If you'd been like some chaps and gone abroad, where would you have been now? Where would have been the reward of your faithful heart?"

Mr. Clarkson, whose pipe had gone out, took a coal from the fire and lit it again.

"I can't understand him dying at his age," he said, darkly. "He ought to have lived to ninety if he'd been taken care of."

"Well, he's gone, pore chap," said his friend. "What a blessing it must ha' been to him in his last moments to think that he had made provision for his wife."

"Provision!" exclaimed Mr. Clarkson. "Why he's left her nothing but the furniture and fifty pounds insurance money—nothing in the world."

Mr. Smithson fidgeted. "I mean you," he said, staring.

"Oh!" said the other. "Oh, yes—yes, of course."

"And he doesn't want you to eat your heart out in waiting," said Mr. Smithson. "'Never mind about me,' he said to her; 'you go and make Bob happy.' Wonderful pretty girl she used to be, didn't she?" Mr. Clarkson assented.

"And I've no doubt she looks the same to you as ever she did," pursued the sentimental Mr. Smithson. "That's the extraordinary part of it."

Mr. Clarkson turned and eyed him; removed the pipe from his mouth, and, after hesitating a moment, replaced it with a jerk.

"She says she'd rather be faithful to his memory," continued the persevering Mr. Smithson, "but his wishes are her law. She said so to my missis only yesterday."

"Still, she ought to be considered," said Mr. Clarkson, shaking his head. "I think that somebody ought to put it to her. She has got her feelings, poor thing, and, if she would rather not marry again, she oughtn't to be compelled to."

"Just what my missis did say to her," said the other; "but she didn't pay much attention. She said it was Henry's wish and she didn't care what happened to her now he's gone. Besides, if you come to think of it, what else is she to do? Don't you worry, Bob; you won't lose her again."

Mr. Clarkson, staring at the fire, mused darkly. For thirty years he had played the congenial part of the disappointed admirer but faithful friend. He had intended to play it for at least fifty or sixty. He wished that he had had the strength of mind to refuse the bequest when the late Mr. Phipps first mentioned it, or taken a firmer line over the congratulations of his friends. As it was, Little Molton quite understood that after thirty years' waiting the faithful heart was to be rewarded at last. Public opinion seemed to be that the late Mr. Phipps had behaved with extraordinary generosity.

"It's rather late in life for me to begin," said Mr. Clarkson at last.

"Better late than never," said the cheerful Mr. Smithson.

"And something seems to tell me that I ain't long for this world," continued Mr. Clarkson, eyeing him with some disfavour.

"Stuff and nonsense," said Mr. Smithson. "You'll lose all them ideas as soon as you're married. You'll have somebody to look after you and help you spend your money."

Mr. Clarkson emitted a dismal groan, and clapping his hand over his mouth strove to make it pass muster as a yawn. It was evident that the malicious Mr. Smithson was deriving considerable pleasure from his discomfiture—the pleasure natural to the father of seven over the troubles of a comfortable bachelor. Mr. Clarkson, anxious to share his troubles with somebody, came to a sudden and malicious determination to share them with Mr. Smithson.

"I don't want anybody to help me spend my money," he said, slowly. "First and last I've saved a tidy bit. I've got this house, those three cottages in Turner's Lane, and pretty near six hundred pounds in the bank."

Mr. Smithson's eyes glistened.

"I had thought—it had occurred to me," said Mr. Clarkson, trying to keep as near the truth as possible, "to leave my property to a friend o' mine —a hard-working man with a large family. However, it's no use talking about that now. It's too late."

"Who—who was it?" inquired his friend, trying to keep his voice steady.

Mr. Clarkson shook his head. "It's no good talking about that now, George," he said, eyeing him with sly enjoyment. "I shall have to leave everything to my wife now. After all, perhaps it does more harm than good to leave money to people."

"Rubbish!" said Mr. Smithson, sharply. "Who was it?"

"You, George," said Mr. Clarkson, softly.

"Me?" said the other, with a gasp. "Me?" He jumped up from his chair, and, seizing the other's hand, shook it fervently.

"I oughtn't to have told you, George," said Mr. Clarkson, with great satisfaction. "It'll only make you miserable. It's just one o' the might ha' beens."

Mr. Smithson, with his back to the fire and his hands twisted behind him, stood with his eyes fixed in thought.

"It's rather cool of Phipps," he said, after a long silence; "rather cool, I think, to go out of the world and just leave his wife to you to look after. Some men wouldn't stand it. You're too easy-going, Bob, that's what's the matter with you."

Mr. Clarkson sighed.

"And get took advantage of," added his friend.

"It's all very well to talk," said Mr. Clarkson, "but what can I do? I ought to have spoke up at the time. It's too late now."

"If I was you," said his friend very earnestly, "and didn't want to marry her, I should tell her so. Say what you like it ain't fair to her you know. It ain't fair to the pore woman. She'd never forgive you if she found it out."

"Everybody's taking it for granted," said the other.

"Let everybody look after their own business," said Mr. Smithson, tartly. "Now, look here, Bob; suppose I get you out of this business, how am I to be sure you'll leave your property to me?—not that I want it. Suppose you altered your will?"

"If you get me out of it, every penny I leave will go to you," said Mr. Clarkson, fervently. "I haven't got any relations, and it don't matter in the slightest to me who has it after I'm gone."

"As true as you stand there?" demanded the other, eyeing him fixedly.

"As true as I stand here," said Mr. Clarkson, smiting his chest, and shook hands again.

Long after his visitor had gone he sat gazing in a brooding fashion at the fire. As a single man his wants were few, and he could live on his savings; as the husband of Mrs. Phipps he would be compelled to resume the work he thought he had dropped for good three years before. Moreover, Mrs. Phipps possessed a strength of character that had many times caused him to congratulate himself upon her choice of a husband.

Slowly but surely his fetters were made secure. Two days later the widow departed to spend six weeks with a sister; but any joy that he might have felt over the circumstance was marred by the fact that he had to carry her bags down to the railway station and see her off. The key of her house was left with him, with strict injunctions to go in and water her geraniums every day, while two canaries and a bullfinch had to be removed to his own house in order that they might have constant attention and company.

"She's doing it on purpose," said Mr. Smithson, fiercely; "she's binding you hand and foot."

Mr. Clarkson assented gloomily. "I'm trusting to you, George," he remarked.

"How'd it be to forget to water the geraniums and let the birds die because they missed her so much?" suggested Mr. Smithson, after prolonged thought.

Mr. Clarkson shivered.

"It would be a hint," said his friend.

Mr. Clarkson took some letters from the mantelpiece and held them up. "She writes about them every day," he said, briefly, "and I have to answer them."

"She—she don't refer to your getting married, I suppose?" said his friend, anxiously.

Mr. Clarkson said "No. But her sister does," he added. "I've had two letters from her."

Mr. Smithson got up and paced restlessly up and down the room. "That's women all over," he said, bitterly. "They never ask for things straight out; but they always get 'em in roundabout ways. She can't do it herself, so she gets her sister to do it."

Mr. Clarkson groaned. "And her sister is hinting that she can't leave the house where she spent so many happy years," he said, "and says what a pleasant surprise it would be for Mrs. Phipps if she was to come home and find it done up."

"That means you've got to live there when you're married," said his friend, solemnly.

Mr. Clarkson glanced round his comfortable room and groaned again. "She asked me to get an estimate from Digson," he said, dully. "She knows as well as I do her sister hasn't got any money. I wrote to say that it had better be left till she comes home, as I might not know what was wanted."

Mr. Smithson nodded approval.

"And Mrs. Phipps wrote herself and thanked me for being so considerate," continued his friend, grimly, "and says that when she comes back we must go over the house together and see what wants doing."

Mr. Smithson got up and walked round the room again.

"You never promised to marry her?" he said, stopping suddenly.

"No," said the other. "It's all been arranged for me. I never said a word. I couldn't tell Phipps I wouldn't have her with them all standing round, and him thinking he was doing me the greatest favour in the world."

"Well, she can't name the day unless you ask her," said the other. "All you've got to do is to keep quiet and not commit yourself. Be as cool as you can, and, just before she comes home, you go off to London on business and stay there as long as possible."

Mr. Clarkson carried out his instructions to the letter, and Mrs. Phipps, returning home at the end of her visit, learned that he had left for London three days before, leaving the geraniums and birds to the care of Mr. Smithson. From the hands of that unjust steward she received two empty bird-cages, together with a detailed account of the manner in which the occupants had effected their escape, and a bullfinch that seemed to be suffering from torpid liver. The condition of the geraniums was ascribed to worms in the pots, frost, and premature decay.

"They go like it sometimes," said Mr. Smithson, "and when they do nothing will save 'em."

Mrs. Phipps thanked him. "It's very kind of you to take so much trouble," she said, quietly; "some people would have lost the cages too while they were about it."

"I did my best," said Mr. Smithson, in a surly voice.

"I know you did," said Mrs. Phipps, thoughtfully, "and I am sure I am much obliged to you. If there is anything of yours I can look after at any time I shall be only too pleased. When did you say Mr. Clarkson was coming back?"

"He don't know," said Mr. Smithson, promptly. "He might be away a month; and then, again, he might be away six. It all depends. You know what business is."

"It's very thoughtful of him," said Mrs. Phipps. "Very."

"Thoughtful!" repeated Mr. Smithson.

"He has gone away for a time out of consideration for me," said the widow. "As things are, it is a little bit awkward for us to meet much at present."

"I don't think he's gone away for that at all," said the other, bluntly.

Mrs. Phipps shook her head. "Ah, you don't know him as well as I do," she said, fondly. "He has gone away on my account, I feel sure."

Mr. Smithson screwed his lips together and remained silent.

"When he feels that it is right and proper for him to come back," pursued Mrs. Phipps, turning her eyes upwards, "he will come. He has left his comfortable home just for my sake, and I shall not forget it."

Mr. Smithson coughed-a short, dry cough, meant to convey incredulity.

"I shall not do anything to this house till he comes back," said Mrs. Phipps. "I expect he would like to have a voice in it. He always used to admire it and say how comfortable it was. Well, well, we never know what is before us."

Mr. Smithson repeated the substance of the interview to Mr. Clarkson by letter, and in the lengthy correspondence that followed kept him posted as to the movements of Mrs. Phipps. By dint of warnings and entreaties he kept the bridegroom-elect in London for three months. By that time Little Molton was beginning to talk.

"They're beginning to see how the land lays," said Mr. Smithson, on the evening of his friend's return, "and if you keep quiet and do as I tell you she'll begin to see it too. As I said before, she can't name the day till you ask her."

Mr. Clarkson agreed, and the following morning, when he called upon Mrs. Phipps at her request, his manner was so distant that she attributed it to ill-health following business worries and the atmosphere of London. In the front parlour Mr. Digson, a small builder and contractor, was busy whitewashing.

"I thought we might as well get on with that," said Mrs. Phipps; "there is only one way of doing whitewashing, and the room has got to be done. To-morrow Mr. Digson will bring up some papers, and, if you'll come round, you can help me choose."

Mr. Clarkson hesitated. "Why not choose 'em yourself?" he said at last.

"Just what I told her," said Mr. Digson, stroking his black beard. "What'll please you will be sure to please him, I says; and if it don't it ought to."

Mr. Clarkson started. "Perhaps you could help her choose," he said, sharply.

Mr. Digson came down from his perch. "Just what I said," he replied. "If Mrs. Phipps will let me advise her, I'll make this house so she won't know it before I've done with it."

"Mr. Digson has been very kind," said Mrs. Phipps, reproachfully.

"Not at all, ma'am," said the builder, softly. "Anything I can do to make you happy or comfortable will be a pleasure to me."

Mr. Clarkson started again, and an odd idea sent his blood dancing. Digson was a widower; Mrs. Phipps was a widow. Could anything be more suitable or desirable?

"Better let him choose," he said. "After all, he ought to be a good judge."

Mrs. Phipps, after a faint protest, gave way, and Mr. Digson, smiling broadly, mounted his perch again.

Mr. Clarkson's first idea was to consult Mr. Smithson; then he resolved to wait upon events. The idea was fantastic to begin with, but, if things did take such a satisfactory turn, he could not help reflecting that it would not be due to any efforts on the part of Mr. Smithson, and he would no longer be under any testamentary obligations to that enterprising gentleman.

By the end of a week he was jubilant. A child could have told Mr. Digson's intentions—and Mrs. Phipps was anything but a child. Mr. Clarkson admitted cheerfully that Mr. Digson was a younger and better-looking man than himself—a more suitable match in every way. And, so far as he could judge, Mrs. Phipps seemed to think so. At any rate, she had ceased to make the faintest allusion to any tie between them. He left her one day painting a door, while the attentive Digson guided the brush, and walked homewards smiling.

"Morning!" said a voice behind him.

"Morning, Bignell," said Mr. Clarkson.

"When—when is it to be?" inquired his friend, walking beside him.

Mr. Clarkson frowned. "When is what to be?" he demanded, disagreeably.

Mr. Bignell lowered his voice. "You'll lose her if you ain't careful," he said. "Mark my words. Can't you see Digson's little game?"

Mr. Clarkson shrugged his shoulders.

"He's after her money," said the other, with a cautious glance around.

"Money?" said the other, with an astonished laugh. "Why, she hasn't got any."

"Oh, all right," said Mr. Bignell. "You know best of course. I was just giving you the tip, but if you know better—why, there's nothing more to be said. She'll be riding in her carriage and pair in six months, anyhow; the richest woman in Little Molton."

Mr. Clarkson stopped short and eyed him in perplexity.

"Digson got a bit sprung one night and told me," said Mr. Bignell. "She don't know it herself yet—uncle on her mother's side in America. She might know at any moment."

"But—but how did Digson know?" inquired the astonished Mr. Clarkson.

"He wouldn't tell me," was the reply. "But it's good enough for him. What do you think he's after? Her? And mind, don't let on to a soul that I told you."

He walked on, leaving Mr. Clarkson standing in a dazed condition in the centre of the foot-path. Recovering himself by an effort, he walked slowly away, and, after prowling about for some time in an aimless fashion, made his way back to Mrs. Phipps's house.

He emerged an hour later an engaged man, with the date of the wedding fixed. With jaunty steps he walked round and put up the banns, and then, with the air of a man who has completed a successful stroke of business, walked homewards.

Little Molton is a small town and news travels fast, but it did not travel faster than Mr. Smithson as soon as he had heard it. He burst into Mr. Clarkson's room like the proverbial hurricane, and, gasping for breath, leaned against the table and pointed at him an incriminating finger.

"You you've been running," said Mr. Clarkson, uneasily.

"What—what—what do you—mean by it?" gasped Mr. Smithson. "After all my trouble. After our—bargain."

"I altered my mind," said Mr. Clarkson, with dignity.

"Pah!" said the other.

"Just in time," said Mr. Clarkson, speaking rapidly. "Another day and I believe I should ha' been too late. It took me pretty near an hour to talk her over. Said I'd been neglecting her, and all that sort of thing; said that she was beginning to think I didn't want her. As hard a job as ever I had in my life."

"But you didn't want her," said the amazed Mr. Smithson. "You told me so."

"You misunderstood me," said Mr. Clarkson, coughing. "You jump at conclusions."

Mr. Smithson sat staring at him. "I heard," he said at last, with an effort... "I heard that Digson was paying her attentions."

Mr. Clarkson spoke without thought. "Ha, he was only after her money," he said, severely. "Good heavens! What's the matter?"

Mr. Smithson, who had sprung to his feet, made no reply, but stood for some time incapable of speech.

"What—is—the—matter?" repeated Mr. Clarkson. "Ain't you well?"

Mr. Smithson swayed a little, and sank slowly back into his chair again.

"Room's too hot," said his astonished host.

Mr. Smithson, staring straight before him, nodded.

"As I was saying," resumed Mr. Clarkson, in the low tones of confidence, "Digson was after her money. Of course her money don't make any difference to me, although, perhaps, I may be able to do something for friends like you. It's from an uncle in America on her mother's—"

Mr. Smithson made a strange moaning noise, and, snatching his hat from the table, clapped it on his head and made for the door. Mr. Clarkson flung his arms around him and dragged him back by main force.

"What are you carrying on like that for?" he demanded. "What do you mean by it?"

"Fancy!" returned Mr. Smithson, with intense bitterness. "I thought Digson was the biggest fool in the place, and I find I've made a mistake. So have you. Good-night."

He opened the door and dashed out. Mr. Clarkson, with a strange sinking at his heart, watched him up the road.

BILL'S LAPSE

Strength and good-nature—said the night-watchman, musingly, as he felt his biceps—strength and good-nature always go together. Sometimes you find a strong man who is not good-natured, but then, as everybody he comes in contack with is, it comes to the same thing.

The strongest and kindest-'earted man I ever come across was a man o' the name of Bill Burton, a ship-mate of Ginger Dick's. For that matter 'e was a shipmate o' Peter Russet's and old Sam Small's too. Not over and above tall; just about my height, his arms was like another man's legs for size, and 'is chest and his back and shoulders might ha' been made for a giant. And with all that he'd got a soft blue eye like a gal's (blue's my favourite colour for gals' eyes), and a nice, soft, curly brown beard. He was an A.B., too, and that showed 'ow good-natured he was, to pick up with firemen.

He got so fond of 'em that when they was all paid off from the *Ocean King* he asked to be allowed to join them in taking a room ashore. It pleased every-body, four coming cheaper than three, and Bill being that good-tempered that 'e'd put up with anything, and when any of the three quarrelled he used to act the part of peacemaker.

The only thing about 'im that they didn't like was that 'e was a teetotaler. He'd go into public-'ouses with 'em, but he wouldn't drink; leastways, that is to say, he wouldn't drink beer, and Ginger used to say that it made 'im feel uncomfortable to see Bill put away a bottle o' lemonade every time they 'ad a drink. One night arter 'e had 'ad seventeen bottles he could 'ardly got home, and Peter Russet, who knew a lot about pills and such-like, pointed out to 'im 'ow bad it was for his constitushon. He proved that the lemonade would eat away the coats o' Bill's stomach, and that if 'e kept on 'e might drop down dead at any moment.

That frightened Bill a bit, and the next night, instead of 'aving lemonade, 'e had five bottles o' stone ginger-beer, six of different kinds of teetotal beer, three of soda-water, and two cups of coffee. I'm not counting the drink he 'ad at the chemist's shop arterward, because he took that as medicine, but he was so queer in 'is inside next morning that 'e began to be afraid he'd 'ave to give up drink altogether.

He went without the next night, but 'e was such a generous man that 'e would pay every fourth time, and there was no pleasure to the other chaps to see 'im pay and 'ave nothing out of it. It spoilt their evening, and owing to 'aving only about 'arf wot they was accustomed to they all got up very disagreeable next morning.

"Why not take just a little beer, Bill?" asks Ginger.

Bill 'ung his 'ead and looked a bit silly. "I'd rather not, mate," he ses, at last. "I've been teetotal for eleven months now."

"Think of your 'ealth, Bill," ses Peter Russet; "your 'ealth is more important than the pledge. Wot made you take it?"

Bill coughed. "I 'ad reasons," he ses, slowly. "A mate o' mine wished me to."

"He ought to ha' known better," ses Sam. "He 'ad 'is reasons," ses Bill.

"Well, all I can say is, Bill," ses Ginger, "all I can say is, it's very disobligin' of you."

"Disobligin'?" ses Bill, with a start; "don't say that, mate."

"I must say it," ses Ginger, speaking very firm.

"You needn't take a lot, Bill," ses Sam; "nobody wants you to do that. Just drink in moderation, same as wot we do."

"It gets into my 'ead," ses Bill, at last.

"Well, and wot of it?" ses Ginger; "it gets into everybody's 'ead occasionally. Why, one night old Sam 'ere went up behind a policeman and tickled 'im under the arms; didn't you, Sam?"

"I did nothing o' the kind," ses Sam, firing up.

"Well, you was fined ten bob for it next morning, that's all I know," ses Ginger.

"I was fined ten bob for punching 'im," ses old Sam, very wild. "I never tickled a policeman in my life. I never thought o' such a thing. I'd no more tickle a policeman than I'd fly. Anybody that ses I did is a liar. Why should I? Where does the sense come in? Wot should I want to do it for?"

"All right, Sam," ses Ginger, sticking 'is fingers in 'is ears, "you didn't, then."

"No, I didn't," ses Sam, "and don't you forget it. This ain't the fust time you've told that lie about me. I can take a joke with any man; but anybody that goes and ses I tickled—"

"All right," ses Ginger and Peter Russet together. "You'll 'ave tickled policeman on the brain if you ain't careful, Sam," ses Peter.

Old Sam sat down growling, and Ginger Dick turned to Bill agin. "It gets into everybody's 'ead at times," he ses, "and where's the 'arm? It's wot it was meant for."

Bill shook his 'ead, but when Ginger called 'im disobligin' agin he gave way and he broke the pledge that very evening with a pint o' six 'arf.

Ginger was surprised to see the way 'e took his liquor. Arter three or four pints he'd expected to see 'im turn a bit silly, or sing, or do something o' the kind, but Bill kept on as if 'e was drinking water.

"Think of the 'armless pleasure you've been losing all these months, Bill," ses Ginger, smiling at him.

Bill said it wouldn't bear thinking of, and, the next place they came to he said some rather 'ard things of the man who'd persuaded 'im to take the pledge. He 'ad two or three more there, and then they began to see that it was beginning to have an effect on 'im. The first one that noticed it was Ginger Dick. Bill 'ad just lit 'is pipe, and as he threw the match down he ses: "I don't like these 'ere safety matches," he ses.

"Don't you, Bill?" ses Ginger. "I do, rather."

"Oh, you do, do you?" ses Bill, turning on 'im like lightning; "well, take that for contradictin'," he ses, an' he gave Ginger a smack that nearly knocked his 'ead off.

It was so sudden that old Sam and Peter put their beer down and stared at each other as if they couldn't believe their eyes. Then they stooped down and helped pore Ginger on to 'is legs agin and began to brush 'im down.

"Never mind about 'im, mates," ses Bill, looking at Ginger very wicked. "P'r'aps he won't be so ready to give me 'is lip next time. Let's come to another pub and enjoy ourselves."

Sam and Peter followed 'im out like lambs, 'ardly daring to look over their shoulder at Ginger, who was staggering arter them some distance behind a 'olding a handerchief to 'is face.

"It's your turn to pay, Sam," ses Bill, when they'd got inside the next place. "Wot's it to be? Give it a name."

"Three 'arf pints o' four ale, miss," ses Sam, not because 'e was mean, but because it wasn't 'is turn. "Three wot?" ses Bill, turning on 'im.

"Three pots o' six ale, miss," ses Sam, in a hurry.

"That wasn't wot you said afore," ses Bill. "Take that," he ses, giving pore old Sam a wipe in the mouth and knocking 'im over a stool; "take that for your sauce."

Peter Russet stood staring at Sam and wondering wot Bill ud be like when he'd 'ad a little more. Sam picked hisself up arter a time and went outside to talk to Ginger about it, and then Bill put 'is arm round Peter's neck and began to cry a bit and say 'e was the only pal he'd got left in the world. It was very awkward for Peter, and more awkward still when the barman came up and told 'im to take Bill outside.

"Go on," he ses, "out with 'im."

"He's all right," ses Peter, trembling; "we's the truest-'arted gentleman in London. Ain't you, Bill?"

Bill said he was, and 'e asked the barman to go and hide 'is face because it reminded 'im of a little dog 'e had 'ad once wot 'ad died.

"You get outside afore you're hurt," ses the bar-man.

Bill punched at 'im over the bar, and not being able to reach 'im threw Peter's pot o' beer at 'im. There was a fearful to-do then, and the landlord jumped over the bar and stood in the doorway, whistling for the police. Bill struck out right and left, and the men in the bar went down like skittles, Peter among them. Then they got outside, and Bill, arter giving the landlord a thump in the back wot nearly made him swallow the whistle, jumped into a cab and pulled Peter Russet in arter 'im.

"I'll talk to you by-and-by," he ses, as the cab drove off at a gallop; "there ain't room in this cab. You wait, my lad, that's all. You just wait till we get out, and I'll knock you silly."

"Wot for, Bill?" ses Peter, staring.

"Don't you talk to me," roars Bill. "If I choose to knock you about that's my business, ain't it? Besides, you know very well."

He wouldn't let Peter say another word, but coming to a quiet place near the docks he stopped the cab and pulling 'im out gave 'im such a dressing down that Peter thought 'is last hour 'ad arrived. He let 'im go at last, and after first making him pay the cab-man took 'im along till they came to a public-'ouse and made 'im pay for drinks.

They stayed there till nearly eleven o'clock, and then Bill set off home 'olding the unfortunit Peter by the scruff o' the neck, and wondering out loud whether 'e ought to pay 'im a bit more or not. Afore 'e could make up 'is mind, however, he turned sleepy, and, throwing 'imself down on the bed which was meant for the two of 'em, fell into a peaceful sleep.

Sam and Ginger Dick came in a little while arterward, both badly marked where Bill 'ad hit them, and sat talking to Peter in whispers as to wot was to be done. Ginger, who 'ad plenty of pluck, was for them all to set on to 'im, but Sam wouldn't 'ear of it, and as for Peter he was so sore he could 'ardly move.

They all turned in to the other bed at last, 'arf afraid to move for fear of disturbing Bill, and when they woke up in the morning and see 'im sitting up in 'is bed they lay as still as mice.

"Why, Ginger, old chap," ses Bill, with a 'earty smile, "wot are you all three in one bed for?" "We was a bit cold," ses Ginger.

"Cold?" ses Bill. "Wot, this weather? We 'ad a bit of a spree last night, old man, didn't we? My throat's as dry as a cinder."

"It ain't my idea of a spree," ses Ginger, sitting up and looking at 'im.

"Good 'eavens, Ginger!" ses Bill, starting back, "wotever 'ave you been a-doing to your face? Have you been tumbling off of a 'bus?"

Ginger couldn't answer; and Sam Small and Peter sat up in bed alongside of 'im, and Bill, getting as far back on 'is bed as he could, sat staring at their pore faces as if 'e was having a 'orrible dream.

"And there's Sam," he ses. "Where ever did you get that mouth, Sam?"

"Same place as Ginger got 'is eye and pore Peter got 'is face," ses Sam, grinding his teeth.

"You don't mean to tell me," ses Bill, in a sad voice—"you don't mean to tell me that I did it?"

"You know well enough," ses Ginger.

Bill looked at 'em, and 'is face got as long as a yard measure.

"I'd 'oped I'd growed out of it, mates," he ses, at last, "but drink always takes me like that. I can't keep a pal."

"You surprise me," ses Ginger, sarcastic-like. "Don't talk like that, Ginger," ses Bill, 'arf crying.

"It ain't my fault; it's my weakness. Wot did I do it for?"

"I don't know," ses Ginger, "but you won't get the chance of doing it agin, I'll tell you that much."

"I daresay I shall be better to-night, Ginger," ses Bill, very humble; "it don't always take me that way.

"Well, we don't want you with us anymore," ses old Sam, 'olding his 'ead very high.

"You'll 'ave to go and get your beer by yourself, Bill," ses Peter Russet, feeling 'is bruises with the tips of 'is fingers.

"But then I should be worse," ses Bill. "I want cheerful company when I'm like that. I should very likely come 'ome and 'arf kill you all in your beds. You don't 'arf know what I'm like. Last night was nothing, else I should 'ave remembered it."

"Cheerful company?" ses old Sam. 'Ow do you think company's going to be cheerful when you're carrying on like that, Bill? Why don't you go away and leave us alone?"

"Because I've got a 'art," ses Bill. "I can't chuck up pals in that free-and-easy way. Once I take a liking to anybody I'd do anything for 'em, and I've never met three chaps I like better than wot I do you. Three nicer, straight-forrad, free-'anded mates I've never met afore."

"Why not take the pledge agin, Bill?" ses Peter Russet.

"No, mate," ses Bill, with a kind smile; "it's just a weakness, and I must try and grow out of it. I'll tie a bit o' string round my little finger to-night as a re-minder."

He got out of bed and began to wash 'is face, and Ginger Dick, who was doing a bit o' thinking, gave a whisper to Sam and Peter Russet.

"All right, Bill, old man," he ses, getting out of bed and beginning to put his clothes on; "but first of all we'll try and find out 'ow the landlord is."

"Landlord?" ses Bill, puffing and blowing in the basin. "Wot landlord?"

"Why, the one you bashed," ses Ginger, with a wink at the other two. "He 'adn't got 'is senses back when me and Sam came away."

Bill gave a groan and sat on the bed while 'e dried himself, and Ginger told 'im 'ow he 'ad bent a quart pot on the landlord's 'ead, and 'ow the landlord 'ad been carried upstairs and the doctor sent for. He began to tremble all over, and when Ginger said he'd go out and see 'ow the land lay 'e could 'ardly thank 'im enough.

He stayed in the bedroom all day, with the blinds down, and wouldn't eat anything, and when Ginger looked in about eight o'clock to find out whether he 'ad gone, he found 'im sitting on the bed clean shaved, and 'is face cut about all over where the razor 'ad slipped.

Ginger was gone about two hours, and when 'e came back he looked so solemn that old Sam asked 'im whether he 'ad seen a ghost. Ginger didn't answer 'im; he set down on the side o' the bed and sat thinking.

"I s'pose—I s'pose it's nice and fresh in the streets this morning?" ses Bill, at last, in a trembling voice.

Ginger started and looked at 'im. "I didn't notice, mate," he ses. Then 'e got up and patted Bill on the back, very gentle, and sat down again.

"Anything wrong, Ginger?" asks Peter Russet, staring at 'im.

"It's that landlord," ses Ginger; "there's straw down in the road outside, and they say that he's dying. Pore old Bill don't know 'is own strength. The best thing you can do, old pal, is to go as far away as you can, at once."

"I shouldn't wait a minnit if it was me," ses old Sam.

Bill groaned and hid 'is face in his 'ands, and then Peter Russet went and spoilt things by saying that the safest place for a murderer to 'ide in was London. Bill gave a dreadful groan when 'e said murderer, but 'e up and agreed with Peter, and all Sam and Ginger Dick could do wouldn't make 'im alter his mind. He said that he would shave off 'is beard and moustache, and when night came 'e would creep out and take a lodging somewhere right the other end of London.

"It'll soon be dark," ses Ginger, "and your own brother wouldn't know you now, Bill. Where d'you think of going?"

Bill shook his 'ead. "Nobody must know that, mate," he ses. "I must go into hiding for as long as I can—as long as my money lasts; I've only got six pounds left."

"That'll last a long time if you're careful," ses Ginger.

"I want a lot more," ses Bill. "I want you to take this silver ring as a keepsake, Ginger. If I 'ad another six pounds or so I should feel much safer. 'Ow much 'ave you got, Ginger?"

"Not much," ses Ginger, shaking his 'ead.

"Lend it to me, mate," ses Bill, stretching out his 'and. "You can easy get another ship. Ah, I wish I was you; I'd be as 'appy as 'appy if I hadn't got a penny."

"I'm very sorry, Bill," ses Ginger, trying to smile, "but I've already promised to lend it to a man wot we met this evening. A promise is a promise, else I'd lend it to you with pleasure."

"Would you let me be 'ung for the sake of a few pounds, Ginger?" ses Bill, looking at 'im reproach-fully. "I'm a desprit man, Ginger, and I must 'ave that money."

Afore pore Ginger could move he suddenly clapped 'is hand over 'is mouth and flung 'im on the bed. Ginger was like a child in 'is hands, although he struggled like a madman, and in five minutes 'e was laying there with a towel tied round his mouth and 'is arms and legs tied up with the cord off of Sam's chest.

"I'm very sorry, Ginger," ses Bill, as 'e took a little over eight pounds out of Ginger's pocket. "I'll pay you back one o' these days, if I can. If you'd got a rope round your neck same as I 'ave you'd do the same as I've done."

He lifted up the bedclothes and put Ginger inside and tucked 'im up. Ginger's face was red with passion and 'is eyes starting out of his 'ead.

"Eight and six is fifteen," ses Bill, and just then he 'eard somebody coming up the stairs. Ginger 'eard it, too, and as Peter Russet came into the room 'e tried all 'e could to attract 'is attention by rolling 'is 'ead from side to side.

"Why, 'as Ginger gone to bed?" ses Peter. "Wot's up, Ginger?"

"He's all right," ses Bill; "just a bit of a 'eadache."

Peter stood staring at the bed, and then 'e pulled the clothes off and saw pore Ginger all tied up, and making awful eyes at 'im to undo him.

"I 'ad to do it, Peter," ses Bill. "I wanted some more money to escape with, and 'e wouldn't lend it to me. I 'aven't got as much as I want now. You just came in in the nick of time. Another minute and you'd ha' missed me. 'Ow much 'ave you got?"

"Ah, I wish I could lend you some, Bill," ses Peter Russet, turning pale, "but I've 'ad my pocket picked; that's wot I came back for, to get some from Ginger."

Bill didn't say a word.

"You see 'ow it is, Bill," ses Peter, edging back toward the door; "three men laid 'old of me and took every farthing I'd got."

"Well, I can't rob you, then," ses Bill, catching 'old of 'im. "Whoever's money this is," he ses, pulling a handful out o' Peter's pocket, "it can't be yours. Now, if you make another sound I'll knock your 'ead off afore I tie you up."

"Don't tie me up, Bill," ses Peter, struggling.

"I can't trust you," ses Bill, dragging 'im over to the washstand and taking up the other towel; "turn round."

Peter was a much easier job than Ginger Dick, and arter Bill 'ad done 'im 'e put 'im in alongside o' Ginger and covered 'em up, arter first tying both the gags round with some string to prevent 'em slipping.

"Mind, I've only borrowed it," he ses, standing by the side o' the bed; "but I must say, mates, I'm disappointed in both of you. If either of you 'ad 'ad the misfortune wot I've 'ad, I'd have sold the clothes off my back to 'elp you. And I wouldn't 'ave waited to be asked neither."

He stood there for a minute very sorrowful, and then 'e patted both their 'eads and went downstairs. Ginger and Peter lay listening for a bit, and then they turned their pore bound-up faces to each other and tried to talk with their eyes.

Then Ginger began to wriggle and try and twist the cords off, but 'e might as well 'ave tried to wriggle out of 'is skin. The worst of it was they couldn't make known their intentions to each other, and when Peter Russet leaned over 'im and tried to work 'is gag off by rubbing it up agin 'is nose, Ginger pretty near went crazy with temper. He banged Peter with his 'ead, and Peter banged back, and they kept it up till they'd both got splitting 'eadaches, and at last they gave up in despair and lay in the darkness waiting for Sam.

And all this time Sam was sitting in the Red Lion, waiting for them. He sat there quite patient till twelve o'clock and then walked slowly 'ome, wondering wot 'ad happened and whether Bill had gone.

Ginger was the fust to 'ear 'is foot on the stairs, and as he came into the room, in the darkness, him an' Peter Russet started shaking their bed in a way that scared old Sam nearly to death. He thought it was Bill carrying on agin, and 'e was out o' that door and 'arf-way downstairs afore he stopped to take breath. He stood there trembling for about ten minutes, and then, as nothing 'appened, he walked slowly upstairs agin on tiptoe, and as soon as they heard the door creak Peter and Ginger made that bed do everything but speak.

"Is that you, Bill?" ses old Sam, in a shaky voice, and standing ready to dash downstairs agin.

There was no answer except for the bed, and Sam didn't know whether Bill was dying or whether 'e 'ad got delirium trimmings. All 'e did know was that 'e wasn't going to sleep in that room. He shut the door gently and went downstairs agin, feeling in 'is pocket for a match, and, not finding one, 'e picked out the softest stair 'e could find and, leaning his 'ead agin the banisters, went to sleep.

It was about six o'clock when 'e woke up, and broad daylight. He was stiff and sore all over, and feeling braver in the light 'e stepped softly upstairs and opened the door. Peter and Ginger was waiting for 'im, and as he peeped in 'e saw two things sitting up in bed with their 'air standing up all over like mops and their faces tied up with bandages. He was that startled 'e nearly screamed, and then 'e stepped into the room and stared at 'em as if he couldn't believe 'is eyes.

"Is that you, Ginger?" he ses. "Wot d'ye mean by making sights of yourselves like that? 'Ave you took leave of your senses?"

Ginger and Peter shook their 'eads and rolled their eyes, and then Sam see wot was the matter with 'em. Fust thing 'e did was to pull out 'is knife and cut Ginger's gag off, and the fust thing Ginger did was to call 'im every name 'e could lay his tongue to.

"You wait a moment," he screams, 'arf crying with rage. "You wait till I get my 'ands loose and I'll pull you to pieces. The idea o' leaving us like this all night, you old crocodile. I 'eard you come in. I'll pay you."

Sam didn't answer 'im. He cut off Peter Russet's gag, and Peter Russet called 'im 'arf a score o' names without taking breath.

"And when Ginger's finished I'll 'ave a go at you," he ses. "Cut off these lines."

"At once, d'ye hear?" ses Ginger. "Oh, you wait till I get my 'ands on you."

Sam didn't answer 'em; he shut up 'is knife with a click and then 'e sat at the foot o' the bed on Ginger's feet and looked at 'em. It wasn't the fust time they'd been rude to 'im, but as a rule he'd 'ad to put up with it. He sat and listened while Ginger swore 'imself faint.

"That'll do," he ses, at last; "another word and I shall put the bedclothes over your 'ead. Afore I do anything more I want to know wot it's all about."

Peter told 'im, arter fust calling 'im some more names, because Ginger was past it, and when 'e'd finished old Sam said 'ow surprised he was at them for letting Bill do it, and told 'em how they ought to 'ave prevented it. He sat there talking as though 'e enjoyed the sound of 'is own voice, and he told Peter and Ginger all their faults and said wot sorrow it caused their friends. Twice he 'ad to throw the bedclothes over their 'eads because o' the noise they was making.

"*Are you going—to undo—us?*" ses Ginger, at last.

"No, Ginger," ses old Sam; "in justice to myself I couldn't do it. Arter wot you've said—and arter wot I've said—my life wouldn't be safe. Besides which, you'd want to go shares in my money."

He took up 'is chest and marched downstairs with it, and about 'arf an hour arterward the landlady's 'usband came up and set 'em free. As soon as they'd got the use of their legs back they started out to look for Sam, but they didn't find 'im for nearly a year, and as for Bill, they never set eyes on 'im again.

BILL'S PAPER CHASE

Sailormen 'ave their faults, said the night watchman, frankly. I'm not denying of it. I used to 'ave myself when I was at sea, but being close with their money is a fault as can seldom be brought ag'in 'em.

I saved some money once—two golden sovereigns, owing to a 'ole in my pocket. Before I got another ship I slept two nights on a doorstep and 'ad nothing to eat, and I found them two sovereigns in the lining o' my coat when I was over two thousand miles away from the nearest pub.

I on'y knew one miser all the years I was at sea. Thomas Geary 'is name was, and we was shipmates aboard the barque *Grenada,* homeward bound from Sydney to London.

Thomas was a man that was getting into years; sixty, I think 'e was, and old enough to know better. 'E'd been saving 'ard for over forty years, and as near as we could make out 'e was worth a matter o' six 'undered pounds. He used to be fond o' talking about it, and letting us know how much better off 'e was than any of the rest of us.

We was about a month out from Sydney when old Thomas took sick. Bill Hicks said that it was owing to a ha'penny he couldn't account for; but Walter Jones, whose family was always ill, and thought 'e knew a lot about it, said that 'e knew wot it was, but 'e couldn't remember the name of it, and that when we got to London and Thomas saw a doctor, we should see as 'ow 'e was right.

Whatever it was the old man got worse and worse. The skipper came down and gave 'im some physic and looked at 'is tongue, and then 'e looked at our tongues to see wot the difference was. Then 'e left the cook in charge of 'im and went off.

The next day Thomas was worse, and it was soon clear to everybody but 'im that 'e was slipping 'is cable. He wouldn't believe it at first, though the cook told 'im, Bill Hicks told him, and Walter Jones 'ad a grandfather that went off in just the same way.

"I'm not going to die," says Thomas "How can I die and leave all that money?"

"It'll be good for your relations, Thomas," says Walter Jones.

"I ain't got any," says the old man.

"Well, your friends, then, Thomas," says Walter, soft-like.

"Ain't got any," says the old man ag'in.

"Yes, you 'ave, Thomas," says Walter, with a kind smile; "I could tell you one you've got."

Thomas shut his eyes at 'im and began to talk pitiful about 'is money and the 'ard work 'e'd 'ad saving of it. And by-and-by 'e got worse, and didn't reckernise us, but thought we was a pack o' greedy, drunken sailormen. He thought Walter Jones was a shark, and told 'im so, and, try all 'e could, Walter couldn't persuade 'im different.

He died the day arter. In the morning 'e was whimpering about 'is money ag'in, and angry with Bill when 'e reminded 'im that 'e couldn't take it with 'im, and 'e made Bill promise that 'e should be buried just as 'e was. Bill tucked him up arter that, and when 'e felt a canvas belt tied round the old man's waist 'e began to see wot 'e was driving at.

The weather was dirty that day and there was a bit o' sea running, consequently all 'ands was on deck, and a boy about sixteen wot used to 'elp the steward down aft was lookin' arter Thomas. Me and Bill just run down to give a look at the old man in time.

"I am going to take it with me, Bill," says the old man.

"That's right," says Bill.

"My mind's—easy now," says Thomas. "I gave it to Jimmy—to—to—throw overboard for me."

"Wot?" says Bill, staring.

"That's right, Bill," says the boy. "He told me to. It was a little packet o' banknotes. He gave me tuppence for doing it."

Old Thomas seemed to be listening. 'Is eyes was open, and 'e looked artful at Bill to think what a clever thing 'e'd done.

"Nobody's goin'-to spend-my money," 'e says. "Nobody's"

We drew back from 'is bunk and stood staring at 'im. Then Bill turned to the boy.

"Go and tell the skipper 'e's gone," 'e says, "and mind, for your own sake, don't tell the skipper or anybody else that you've thrown all that money overboard."

"Why not?" says Jimmy.

"Becos you'll be locked up for it," says Bill; "you'd no business to do it. You've been and broke the law. It ought to ha' been left to somebody."

Jimmy looked scared, and arter 'e was gone I turned to Bill, and I looks at 'im and I says "What's the little game, Bill?"

"*Game*?" said Bill, snorting at me. "I don't want the pore boy to get into trouble, do I? Pore little chap. You was young yourself once."

"Yes," I says; "but I'm a bit older now, Bill, and unless you tell me what your little game is, I shall tell the skipper myself, and the chaps too. Pore old Thomas told 'im to do it, so where's the boy to blame?"

"Do you think Jimmy did?" says Bill, screwing up his nose at me. "That little varmint is walking about worth six 'undered quid. Now you keep your mouth shut and I'll make it worth your while."

Then I see Bill's game. "All right, I'll keep quiet for the sake of my half," I says, looking at 'im.

I thought he'd ha' choked, and the langwidge 'e see fit to use was a'most as much as I could answer.

"Very well, then," 'e says, at last, "halves it is. It ain't robbery becos it belongs to nobody, and it ain't the boy's becos 'e was told to throw it overboard."

They buried pore old Thomas next morning, and arter it was all over Bill put 'is 'and on the boy's shoulder as they walked for'ard and 'e says, "Poor old Thomas 'as gone to look for 'is money," he says; "wonder whether 'e'll find it! Was it a big bundle, Jimmy?"

"No," says the boy, shaking 'is 'ead. "They was six 'undered pound notes and two sovereigns, and I wrapped the sovereigns up in the notes to make 'em sink. Fancy throwing money away like that, Bill: seems a sin, don't it?"

Bill didn't answer 'im, and that afternoon the other chaps below being asleep we searched 'is bunk through and through without any luck, and at last Bill sat down and swore 'e must ha' got it about 'im.

We waited till night, and when everybody was snoring 'ard we went over to the boy's bunk and went all through 'is pockets and felt the linings, and then we went back to our side and Bill said wot 'e thought about Jimmy in whispers.

"He must ha' got it tied round 'is waist next to 'is skin, like Thomas 'ad," I says.

We stood there in the dark whispering, and then Bill couldn't stand it any longer, and 'e went over on tiptoe to the bunk ag'in. He was tremblin' with excitement and I wasn't much better, when all of a sudden the cook sat up in 'is bunk with a dreadful laughing scream and called out that somebody was ticklin' 'im.

I got into my bunk and Bill got into 'is, and we lay there listening while the cook, who was a terrible ticklish man, leaned out of 'is bunk and said wot 'e'd do if it 'appened ag'in.

"Go to sleep," says Walter Jones; "you're dreamin'. Who d'you think would want to tickle you?"

"I tell you," says the cook, "somebody come over and tickled me with a 'and the size of a leg o' mutton. I feel creepy all over."

Bill gave it up for that night, but the next day 'e pretended to think Jimmy was gettin' fat an' 'e caught 'old of 'im and prodded 'im all over. He thought 'e felt something round 'is waist, but 'e couldn't be sure, and Jimmy made such a noise that the other chaps interfered and told Bill to leave 'im alone. For a whole week we tried to find that money, and couldn't, and Bill said it was a suspicious thing that Jimmy kept aft a good deal more than 'e used to, and 'e got an idea that the boy might ha' 'idden it somewhere there. At the end of that time, 'owever, owing to our being short-'anded, Jimmy was sent for'ard to work as ordinary seaman, and it began to be quite noticeable the way 'e avoided Bill.

At last one day we got 'im alone down the fo'c'sle, and Bill put 'is arm round 'im and got im on the locker and asked 'im straight out where the money was.

"Why, I chucked it overboard," he says. "I told you so afore. What a memory you've got, Bill!"

Bill picked 'im up and laid 'im on the locker, and we searched 'im thoroughly. We even took 'is boots off, and then we 'ad another look in 'is bunk while 'e was putting 'em on ag'in.

"If you're innercent," says Bill, "why don't you call out?—eh?"

"Because you told me not to say anything about it, Bill," says the boy. "But I will next time. Loud, I will."

"Look 'ere," says Bill, "you tell us where it is, and the three of us'll go shares in it. That'll be two 'undered pounds each, and we'll tell you 'ow to get yours changed without getting caught. We're cleverer than you are, you know."

"I know that, Bill," says the boy; "but it's no good me telling you lies. I chucked it overboard."

"Very good, then," says Bill, getting up. "I'm going to tell the skipper."

"Tell 'im," says Jimmy. "I don't care."

"Then you'll be searched arter you've stepped ashore," says Bill, "and you won't be allowed on the ship ag'in. You'll lose it all by being greedy, whereas if you go shares with us you'll 'ave two 'undered pounds."

I could see as 'ow the boy 'adn't thought o' that, and try as 'e would 'e couldn't 'ide 'is feelin's. He called Bill a red-nosed shark, and 'e called me somethin' I've forgotten now.

"Think it over," says Bill; "mind, you'll be collared as soon as you've left the gangway and searched by the police."

"And will they tickle the cook too, I wonder?" says Jimmy, savagely.

"And if they find it you'll go to prison," says Bill, giving 'im a clump o' the side o' the 'ead, "and you won't like that, I can tell you."

"Why, ain't it nice, Bill?" says Jimmy, holding 'is ear.

Bill looked at 'im and then 'e steps to the ladder. "I'm not going to talk to you any more, my lad," 'e says. "I'm going to tell the skipper."

He went up slowly, and just as 'e reached the deck Jimmy started up and called 'im. Bill pretended not to 'ear, and the boy ran up on deck and follered 'im; and arter a little while they both came down again together.

"Did you wish to speak to me, my lad?" says Bill, 'olding 'is 'ead up.

"Yes," says the boy, fiddling with 'is fingers; "if you keep your ugly mouth shut, we'll go shares."

"Ho!" says Bill, "I thought you throwed it overboard!"

"I thought so, too, Bill," says Jimmy, very softly, "and when I came below ag'in I found it in my trousers pocket."

"Where is it now?" says Bill.

"Never mind where it is," says the boy; "you couldn't get it if I was to tell you. It'll take me all my time to do it myself."

"Where is it?" says Bill, ag'in. "I'm goin' to take care of it. I won't trust you."

"And I can't trust you," says Jimmy.

"If you don't tell me where it is this minute," says Bill, moving to the ladder ag'in, "I'm off to tell the skipper. I want it in my 'ands, or at any rate my share of it. Why not share it out now?"

"Because I 'aven't got it," says Jimmy, stamping 'is foot, "that's why, and it's all your silly fault. Arter you came pawing through my pockets when you thought I was asleep I got frightened and 'id it."

"Where?" says Bill.

"In the second mate's mattress," says Jimmy. "I was tidying up down aft and I found a 'ole in the underneath side of 'is mattress and I shoved it in there, and poked it in with a bit o' stick."

"And 'ow are you going to get it?" says Bill, scratching 'is 'ead.

"That's wot I don't know, seeing that I'm not allowed aft now," says Jimmy. "One of us'll 'ave to make a dash for it when we get to London. And mind if there's any 'ankypanky on your part, Bill, I'll give the show away myself."

The cook came down just then and we 'ad to leave off talking, and I could see that Bill was so pleased at finding that the money 'adn't been thrown overboard that 'e was losing sight o' the difficulty o' getting at it. In a day or two, 'owever, 'e see it as plain as me and Jimmy did, and, as time went by, he got desprit, and frightened us both by 'anging about aft every chance 'e got.

The companion-way faced the wheel, and there was about as much chance o' getting down there without being seen as there would be o' taking a man's false teeth out of 'is mouth without 'is knowing it. Jimmy went down one day while Bill was at the wheel to look for 'is knife, wot 'e thought 'e'd left down there, and 'ed 'ardly got down afore Bill saw 'im come up ag'in, 'olding on to the top of a mop which the steward was using.

We couldn't figure it out nohow, and to think o' the second mate, a little man with a large fam'ly, who never 'ad a penny in 'is pocket, sleeping every night on a six 'undered pound mattress, sent us pretty near crazy. We used to talk it over whenever we got a chance, and Bill and Jimmy could scarcely be civil to each other. The boy said it was Bill's fault, and 'e said it was the boy's.

"The on'y thing I can see," says the boy, one day, "is for Bill to 'ave a touch of sunstroke as 'e's leaving the wheel one day, tumble 'ead-first down the companion-way, and injure 'isself so severely that 'e can't be moved. Then they'll put 'im in a cabin down aft, and p'raps I'll 'ave to go and nurse 'im. Anyway, he'll be down there."

"It's a very good idea, Bill," I says.

"Ho," says Bill, looking at me as if 'e would eat me. "Why don't you do it, then?"

"I'd sooner you did it, Bill," says the boy; "still, I don't mind which it is. Why not toss up for it?"

"Get away," says Bill. "Get away afore I do something you won't like, you blood-thirsty little murderer."

"I've got a plan myself," he says, in a low voice, after the boy 'ad 'opped off, "and if I can't think of nothing better I'll try it, and mind, not a word to the boy."

He didn't think o' nothing better, and one night just as we was making the Channel 'e tried 'is plan. He was in the second mate's watch, and by-and-by 'e leans over the wheel and says to 'im in a low voice, "This is my last v'y'ge, sir."

"Oh," says the second mate, who was a man as didn't mind talking to a man before the mast. "How's that?"

"I've got a berth ashore, sir," says Bill, "and I wanted to ask a favour, sir."

The second mate growled and walked off a pace or two.

"I've never been so 'appy as I've been on this ship," says Bill; "none of us 'ave. We was saying so the other night, and everybody agreed as it was owing to you, sir, and your kindness to all of us."

The second mate coughed, but Bill could see as 'e was a bit pleased.

"The feeling came over me," says Bill, "that when I leave the sea for good I'd like to 'ave something o' yours to remember you by, sir. And it seemed to me that if I 'ad your—mattress I should think of you ev'ry night o' my life."

"My wot?" says the second mate, staring at 'im. "Your mattress, sir," says Bill. "If I might make so bold as to offer a pound for it, sir. I want something wot's been used by you, and I've got a fancy for that as a keepsake." The second mate shook 'is 'ead. "I'm sorry, Bill," 'e says, gently, "but I couldn't let it go at that."

"I'd sooner pay thirty shillin's than not 'ave it, sir," says Bill, 'umbly.

"I gave a lot of money for that mattress," says the mate, ag'in. "I forgot 'ow much, but a lot. You don't know 'ow valuable that mattress is."

"I know it's a good one, sir, else you wouldn't 'ave it," says Bill. "Would a couple o' pounds buy it, sir?"

The second mate hum'd and ha'd, but Bill was afeard to go any 'igher. So far as 'e could make out from Jimmy, the mattress was worth about eighteen pence—to anybody who wasn't pertiklar.

"I've slept on that mattress for years," says the second mate, looking at 'im from the corner of 'is eye. "I don't believe I could sleep on another. Still, to oblige you, Bill, you shall 'ave it at that if you don't want it till we go ashore?"

"Thankee, sir," says Bill, 'ardly able to keep from dancing, "and I'll 'and over the two pounds when we're paid off. I shall keep it all my life, sir, in memory of you and your kindness."

"And mind you keep quiet about it," says the second mate, who didn't want the skipper to know wot 'e'd been doing, "because I don't want to be bothered by other men wanting to buy things as keepsakes."

Bill promised 'im like a shot, and when 'e told me about it 'e was nearly crying with joy.

"And mind," 'e says, "I've bought that mattress, bought it as it stands, and it's got nothing to do with Jimmy. We'll each pay a pound and halve wot's in it."

He persuaded me at last, but that boy watched us like a cat watching a couple of canaries, and I could see we should 'ave all we could do to deceive 'im. He seemed more suspicious o' Bill than me, and 'e kep' worrying us nearly every day to know what we were going to do.

We beat about in the channel with a strong 'ead-wind for four days, and then a tug picked us up and towed us to London.

The excitement of that last little bit was 'orrible. Fust of all we 'ad got to get the mattress, and then in some way we 'ad got to get rid o' Jimmy. Bill's idea was for me to take 'im ashore with me and tell 'im that Bill would join us arterwards, and then lose 'im; but I said that till I'd got my share I couldn't bear to lose sight o' Bill's honest face for 'alf a second.

And, besides, Jimmy wouldn't 'ave gone.

All the way up the river 'e stuck to Bill, and kept asking 'im wot we were to do. 'E was 'alf crying, and so excited that Bill was afraid the other chaps would notice it.

We got to our berth in the East India Docks at last, and arter we were made fast we went below to 'ave a wash and change into our shoregoing togs. Jimmy watched us all the time, and then 'e comes up to Bill biting 'is nails, and says:

"How's it to be done, Bill?"

"Hang about arter the rest 'ave gone ashore, and trust to luck," says Bill, looking at me. "We'll see 'ow the land lays when we draw our advance."

We went down aft to draw ten shillings each to go ashore with. Bill and me got ours fust, and then the second mate who 'ad tipped 'im the wink followed us out unconcerned-like and 'anded Bill the mattress rolled up in a sack.

"'Ere you are, Bill," 'e says.

"Much obliged, sir," says Bill, and 'is 'ands trembled so as 'e could 'ardly 'old it, and 'e made to go off afore Jimmy come on deck.

Then that fool of a mate kept us there while 'e made a little speech. Twice Bill made to go off, but 'e put 'is 'and on 'is arm and kept 'im there while 'e told 'im 'ow he'd always tried to be liked by the men, and 'ad generally succeeded, and in the middle of it up popped Master Jimmy.

He gave a start as he saw the bag, and 'is eyes opened wide, and then as we walked forward 'e put 'is arm through Bill's and called 'im all the names 'e could think of.

"You'd steal the milk out of a cat's saucer," 'e says; "but mind, you don't leave this ship till I've got my share."

"I meant it for a pleasant surprise for you, Jimmy," says Bill, trying to smile.

"I don't like your surprises, Bill, so I don't deceive you," says the boy. "Where are you going to open it?"

"I was thinking of opening it in my bunk," says Bill. "The perlice might want to examine it if we took it through the dock. Come on, Jimmy, old man."

"Yes; all right," says the boy, nodding 'is 'ead at 'im. "I'll stay up 'ere. You might forget yourself, Bill, if I trusted myself down there with you alone. You can throw my share up to me, and then you'll leave the ship afore I do. See?"

"Go to blazes," says Bill; and then, seeing that the last chance 'ad gone, we went below, and 'e chucked the bundle in 'is bunk. There was only one chap down there, and arter spending best part o' ten minutes doing 'is hair 'e nodded to us and went off.

Half a minute later Bill cut open the mattress and began to search through the stuffing, while I struck matches and watched 'im. It wasn't a big mattress and there wasn't much stuffing, but we couldn't seem to see that money. Bill went all over it ag'in and ag'in, and then 'e stood up and looked at me and caught 'is breath painful.

"Do you think the mate found it?" 'e says, in a 'usky voice.

We went through it ag'in, and then Bill went half-way up the fo'c's'le ladder and called softly for Jimmy. He called three times, and then, with a sinking sensation in 'is stummick, 'e went up on deck and I follered 'im. The boy was nowhere to be seen. All we saw was the ship's cat 'aving a wash and brush-up afore going ashore, and the skipper standing aft talking to the owner.

We never saw that boy ag'in. He never turned up for 'is box, and 'e didn't show up to draw 'is pay. Everybody else was there, of course, and arter I'd got mine and come outside I see pore Bill with 'is back up ag'in a wall, staring 'ard at the second mate, who was looking at 'im with a kind smile, and asking 'im 'ow he'd slept. The last thing I saw of Bill, the pore chap 'ad got 'is 'ands in 'is trousers pockets, and was trying 'is hardest to smile back.

BLUNDELL'S IMPROVEMENT

Venia Turnbull in a quiet, unobtrusive fashion was enjoying herself. The cool living-room at Turnbull's farm was a delightful contrast to the hot sunshine without, and the drowsy humming of bees floating in at the open window was charged with hints of slumber to the middle-aged. From her seat by the window she watched with amused interest the efforts of her father—kept from his Sunday afternoon nap by the assiduous attentions of her two admirers—to maintain his politeness.

"Father was so pleased to see you both come in," she said, softly; "it's very dull for him here of an afternoon with only me."

"I can't imagine anybody being dull with only you," said Sergeant Dick Daly, turning a bold brown eye upon her.

Mr. John Blundell scowled; this was the third time the sergeant had said the thing that he would have liked to say if he had thought of it.

"I don't mind being dull," remarked Mr. Turnbull, casually.

Neither gentleman made any comment.

"I like it," pursued Mr. Turnbull, longingly; "always did, from a child."

The two young men looked at each other; then they looked at Venia; the sergeant assumed an expression of careless ease, while John Blundell sat his chair like a human limpet. Mr. Turnbull almost groaned as he remembered his tenacity.

"The garden's looking very nice," he said, with a pathetic glance round.

"Beautiful," assented the sergeant. "I saw it yesterday."

"Some o' the roses on that big bush have opened a bit more since then," said the farmer.

Sergeant Daly expressed his gratification, and said that he was not surprised. It was only ten days since he had arrived in the village on a visit to a relative, but in that short space of time he had, to the great discomfort of Mr. Blundell, made himself wonderfully at home at Mr. Turnbull's. To Venia he related strange adventures by sea and land, and on subjects of which he was sure the farmer knew nothing he was a perfect mine of information. He began to talk in low tones to Venia, and the heart of Mr. Blundell sank within him as he noted her interest. Their voices fell to a gentle murmur, and the sergeant's sleek, well-brushed head bent closer to that of his listener. Relieved from his attentions, Mr. Turnbull fell asleep without more ado.

Blundell sat neglected, the unwilling witness of a flirtation he was powerless to prevent. Considering her limited opportunities, Miss Turnbull displayed a proficiency which astonished him. Even the sergeant was amazed, and suspected her of long practice.

"I wonder whether it is very hot outside?" she said, at last, rising and looking out of the window.

"Only pleasantly warm," said the sergeant. "It would be nice down by the water."

"I'm afraid of disturbing father by our talk," said the considerate daughter. "You might tell him we've gone for a little stroll when he wakes," she added, turning to Blundell.

Mr. Blundell, who had risen with the idea of acting the humble but, in his opinion, highly necessary part of chaperon, sat down again and watched blankly from the window until they were out of sight. He was half inclined to think that the exigencies of the case warranted him in arousing the farmer at once.

It was an hour later when the farmer awoke, to find himself alone with Mr. Blundell, a state of affairs for which he strove with some pertinacity to make that aggrieved gentleman responsible.

"Why didn't you go with them?" he demanded. "Because I wasn't asked," replied the other.

Mr. Turnbull sat up in his chair and eyed him disdainfully. "For a great, big chap like you are, John Blundell," he exclaimed, "it's surprising what a little pluck you've got."

"I don't want to go where I'm not wanted," retorted Mr. Blundell.

"That's where you make a mistake," said the other, regarding him severely; "girls like a masterful man, and, instead of getting your own way, you sit down quietly and do as you're told, like a tame— tame—"

"Tame what?" inquired Mr. Blundell, resentfully.

"I don't know," said the other, frankly; "the tamest thing you can think of. There's Daly laughing in his sleeve at you, and talking to Venia about Waterloo and the Crimea as though he'd been there. I thought it was pretty near settled between you."

"So did I," said Mr. Blundell.

"You're a big man, John," said the other, "but you're slow. You're all muscle and no head."

"I think of things afterward," said Blundell, humbly; "generally after I get to bed."

Mr. Turnbull sniffed, and took a turn up and down the room; then he closed the door and came toward his friend again.

"I dare say you're surprised at me being so anxious to get rid of Venia," he said, slowly, "but the fact is I'm thinking of marrying again myself."

"You!" said the startled Mr. Blundell.

"Yes, me," said the other, somewhat sharply. "But she won't marry so long as Venia is at home. It's a secret, because if Venia got to hear of it she'd keep single to prevent it. She's just that sort of girl."

Mr. Blundell coughed, but did not deny it. "Who is it?" he inquired.

"Miss Sippet," was the reply. "She couldn't hold her own for half an hour against Venia."

Mr. Blundell, a great stickler for accuracy, reduced the time to five minutes.

"And now," said the aggrieved Mr. Turnbull, "now, so far as I can see, she's struck with Daly. If she has him it'll be years and years before they can marry. She seems crazy about heroes. She was talking to me the other night about them. Not to put too fine a point on it, she was talking about you."

Mr. Blundell blushed with pleased surprise.

"Said you were not a hero," explained Mr. Turnbull. "Of course, I stuck up for you. I said you'd got too much sense to go putting your life into danger. I said you were a very careful man, and I told her how particular you was about damp sheets. Your housekeeper told me."

"It's all nonsense," said Blundell, with a fiery face. "I'll send that old fool packing if she can't keep her tongue quiet."

"It's very sensible of you, John," said Mr. Turnbull, "and a sensible girl would appreciate it. Instead of that, she only sniffed when I told her how careful you always were to wear flannel next to your skin. She said she liked dare-devils."

"I suppose she thinks Daly is a dare-devil," said the offended Mr. Blundell. "And I wish people wouldn't talk about me and my skin. Why can't they mind their own business?"

Mr. Turnbull eyed him indignantly, and then, sitting in a very upright position, slowly filled his pipe, and declining a proffered match rose and took one from the mantel-piece.

"I was doing the best I could for you," he said, staring hard at the ingrate. "I was trying to make Venia see what a careful husband you would make. Miss Sippet herself is most particular about such things—and Venia seemed to think something of it, because she asked me whether you used a warming-pan."

Mr. Blundell got up from his chair and, without going through the formality of bidding his host good-by, quitted the room and closed the door violently behind him. He was red with rage, and he brooded darkly as he made his way home on the folly of carrying on the traditions of a devoted mother without thinking for himself.

For the next two or three days, to Venia's secret concern, he failed to put in an appearance at the farm—a fact which made flirtation with the sergeant a somewhat uninteresting business. Her sole recompense was the dismay of her father, and for his benefit she dwelt upon the advantages of the Army in a manner that would have made the fortune of a recruiting-sergeant.

"She's just crazy after the soldiers," he said to Mr. Blundell, whom he was trying to spur on to a desperate effort. "I've been watching her close, and I can see what it is now; she's romantic. You're too slow and ordinary for her. She wants somebody more dazzling. She told Daly only yesterday afternoon that she loved heroes. Told it to him to his face. I sat there and heard her. It's a pity you ain't a hero, John."

"Yes," said Mr. Blundell; "then, if I was, I expect she'd like something else."

The other shook his head. "If you could only do something daring," he murmured; "half-kill some-body, or save somebody's life, and let her see you do it. Couldn't you dive off the quay and save some-body's life from drowning?"

"Yes, I could," said Blundell, "if somebody would only tumble in."

"You might pretend that you thought you saw somebody drowning," suggested Mr. Turnbull.

"And be laughed at," said Mr. Blundell, who knew his Venia by heart.

"You always seem to be able to think of objections," complained Mr. Turnbull; "I've noticed that in you before."

"I'd go in fast enough if there was anybody there," said Blundell. "I'm not much of a swimmer, but—"

"All the better," interrupted the other; "that would make it all the more daring."

"And I don't much care if I'm drowned," pursued the younger man, gloomily.

Mr. Turnbull thrust his hands in his pockets and took a turn or two up and down the room. His brows were knitted and his lips pursed. In the presence of this mental stress Mr. Blundell preserved a respectful silence.

"We'll all four go for a walk on the quay on Sunday afternoon," said Mr. Turnbull, at last.

"On the chance?" inquired his staring friend.

"On the chance," assented the other; "it's just possible Daly might fall in."

"He might if we walked up and down five million times," said Blundell, unpleasantly.

"He might if we walked up and down three or four times," said Mr. Turnbull, "especially if you happened to stumble."

"I never stumble," said the matter-of-fact Mr. Blundell. "I don't know anybody more sure-footed than I am."

"Or thick-headed," added the exasperated Mr. Turnbull.

Mr. Blundell regarded him patiently; he had a strong suspicion that his friend had been drinking.

"Stumbling," said Mr. Turnbull, conquering his annoyance with an effort "stumbling is a thing that might happen to anybody. You trip your foot against a stone and lurch up against Daly; he tumbles overboard, and you off with your jacket and dive in off the quay after him. He can't swim a stroke."

Mr. Blundell caught his breath and gazed at him in speechless amaze.

"There's sure to be several people on the quay if it's a fine afternoon," continued his instructor. "You'll have half Dunchurch round you, praising you and patting you on the back—all in front of Venia, mind you. It'll be put in all the papers and you'll get a medal."

"And suppose we are both drowned?" said Mr. Blundell, soberly.

"Drowned? Fiddlesticks !" said Mr. Turnbull. "However, please yourself. If you're afraid—"

"I'll do it," said Blundell, decidedly.

"And mind," said the other, "don't do it as if it's as easy as kissing your fingers; be half-drowned yourself, or at least pretend to be. And when you're on the quay take your time about coming round. Be longer than Daly is; you don't want him to get all the pity."

"All right," said the other.

"After a time you can open your eyes," went on his instructor; "then, if I were you, I should say, 'Good-bye, Venia,' and close 'em again. Work it up affecting, and send messages to your aunts."

"It sounds all right," said Blundell.

"It is all right," said Mr. Turnbull. "That's just the bare idea I've given you. It's for you to improve upon it. You've got two days to think about it."

Mr. Blundell thanked him, and for the next two days thought of little else. Being a careful man he made his will, and it was in a comparatively cheerful frame of mind that he made his way on Sunday afternoon to Mr. Turnbull's.

The sergeant was already there conversing in low tones with Venia by the window, while Mr. Turnbull, sitting opposite in an oaken armchair, regarded him with an expression which would have shocked Iago.

"We were just thinking of having a blow down by the water," he said, as Blundell entered.

"What! a hot day like this?" said Venia.

"I was just thinking how beautifully cool it is in here," said the sergeant, who was hoping for a repetition of the previous Sunday's performance.

"It's cooler outside," said Mr. Turnbull, with a wilful ignoring of facts; "much cooler when you get used to it."

He led the way with Blundell, and Venia and the sergeant, keeping as much as possible in the shade of the dust-powdered hedges, followed. The sun was blazing in the sky, and scarce half-a-dozen people were to be seen on the little curved quay which constituted the usual Sunday afternoon promenade. The water, a dozen feet below, lapped cool and green against the stone sides.

At the extreme end of the quay, underneath the lantern, they all stopped, ostensibly to admire a full-rigged ship sailing slowly by in the distance, but really to effect the change of partners necessary to the after-noon's business. The change gave Mr. Turnbull some trouble ere it was effected, but he was successful at last, and, walking behind the two young men, waited somewhat nervously for developments.

Twice they paraded the length of the quay and nothing happened. The ship was still visible, and, the sergeant halting to gaze at it, the company lost their formation, and he led the complaisant Venia off from beneath her father's very nose.

"You're a pretty manager, you are, John Blundell," said the incensed Mr. Turnbull.

"I know what I'm about," said Blundell, slowly.

"Well, why don't you do it?" demanded the other. "I suppose you are going to wait until there are more people about, and then perhaps some of them will see you push him over."

"It isn't that," said Blundell, slowly, "but you told me to improve on your plan, you know, and I've been thinking out improvements."

"Well?" said the other.

"It doesn't seem much good saving Daly," said Blundell; "that's what I've been thinking. He would be in as much danger as I should, and he'd get as much sympathy; perhaps more."

"Do you mean to tell me that you are backing out of it?" demanded Mr. Turnbull.

"No," said Blundell, slowly, "but it would be much better if I saved somebody else. I don't want Daly to be pitied."

"Bah! you are backing out of it," said the irritated Mr. Turnbull. "You're afraid of a little cold water."

"No, I'm not," said Blundell; "but it would be better in every way to save somebody else. She'll see Daly standing there doing nothing, while I am struggling for my life. I've thought it all out very carefully. I know I'm not quick, but I'm sure, and when I make up my mind to do a thing, I do it. You ought to know that."

"That's all very well," said the other; "but who else is there to push in?"

"That's all right," said Blundell, vaguely. "Don't you worry about that; I shall find somebody."

Mr. Turnbull turned and cast a speculative eye along the quay. As a rule, he had great confidence in Blundell's determination, but on this occasion he had his doubts.

"Well, it's a riddle to me," he said, slowly. "I give it up. It seems— Halloa! Good heavens, be careful. You nearly had me in then."

"Did I?" said Blundell, thickly. "I'm very sorry."

Mr. Turnbull, angry at such carelessness, accepted the apology in a grudging spirit and trudged along in silence. Then he started nervously as a monstrous and unworthy suspicion occurred to him. It was an incredible thing to suppose, but at the same time he felt that there was nothing like being on the safe side, and in tones not quite free from significance he intimated his desire of changing places with his awkward friend.

"It's all right," said Blundell, soothingly.

"I know it is," said Mr. Turnbull, regarding him fixedly; "but I prefer this side. You very near had me over just now."

"I staggered," said Mr. Blundell.

"Another inch and I should have been overboard," said Mr. Turnbull, with a shudder. "That would have been a nice how d'ye do."

Mr. Blundell coughed and looked seaward. "Accidents will happen," he murmured.

They reached the end of the quay again and stood talking, and when they turned once more the sergeant was surprised and gratified at the ease with which he bore off Venia. Mr. Turnbull and Blundell followed some little way behind, and the former gentleman's suspicions were somewhat lulled by finding that his friend made no attempt to take the inside place. He looked about him with interest for a likely victim, but in vain.

"What are you looking at?" he demanded, impatiently, as Blundell suddenly came to a stop and gazed curiously into the harbour.

"Jelly-fish," said the other, briefly. "I never saw such a monster. It must be a yard across."

Mr. Turnbull stopped, but could see nothing, and even when Blundell pointed it out with his finger he had no better success. He stepped forward a pace, and his suspicions returned with renewed vigour as a hand was laid caressingly on his shoulder. The next moment, with a wild shriek, he shot suddenly over the edge and disappeared. Venia and the sergeant, turning hastily, were just in time to see the fountain which ensued on his immersion.

"Oh, save him!" cried Venia.

The sergeant ran to the edge and gazed in helpless dismay as Mr. Turnbull came to the surface and disappeared again. At the same moment Blundell, who had thrown off his coat, dived into the harbour and, rising rapidly to the surface, caught the fast-choking Mr. Turnbull by the collar.

"Keep still," he cried, sharply, as the farmer tried to clutch him; "keep still or I'll let you go."

"Help!" choked the farmer, gazing up at the little knot of people which had collected on the quay.

A stout fisherman who had not run for thirty years came along the edge of the quay at a shambling trot, with a coil of rope over his arm. John Blundell saw him and, mindful of the farmer's warning about kissing of fingers, etc., raised his disengaged arm and took that frenzied gentleman below the surface again. By the time they came up he was very glad for his own sake to catch the line skilfully thrown by the old fisherman and be drawn gently to the side.

"I'll tow you to the steps," said the fisherman; "don't let go o' the line."

Mr. Turnbull saw to that; he wound the rope round his wrist and began to regain his presence of mind as they were drawn steadily toward the steps. Willing hands drew them out of the water and helped them up on to the quay, where Mr. Turnbull, sitting in his own puddle, coughed up salt water and glared ferociously at the inanimate form of Mr. Blundell. Sergeant Daly and another man were rendering what they piously believed to be first aid to the apparently drowned, while the stout fisherman, with both hands to his mouth, was yelling in heart-rending accents for a barrel.

"He—he—push—pushed me in," gasped the choking Mr. Turnbull.

Nobody paid any attention to him; even Venia, seeing that he was safe, was on her knees by the side of the unconscious Blundell.

"He—he's shamming," bawled the neglected Mr. Turnbull.

"Shame!" said somebody, without even looking round.

"He pushed me in," repeated Mr. Turnbull. "He pushed me in."

"Oh, father," said Venia, with a scandalised glance at him, "how can you?"

"Shame!" said the bystanders, briefly, as they, watched anxiously for signs of returning life on the part of Mr. Blundell. He lay still with his eyes closed, but his hearing was still acute, and the sounds of a rapidly approaching barrel trundled by a breathless Samaritan did him more good than anything.

"Good-bye, Venia," he said, in a faint voice; "good-bye."

Miss Turnbull sobbed and took his hand.

"He's shamming," roared Mr. Turnbull, incensed beyond measure at the faithful manner in which Blundell was carrying out his instructions. "He pushed me in."

There was an angry murmur from the bystanders. "Be reasonable, Mr. Turnbull," said the sergeant, somewhat sharply.

"He nearly lost 'is life over you," said the stout fisherman. "As plucky a thing as ever I see. If I 'adn't ha' been 'andy with that there line you'd both ha' been drownded."

"Give—my love—to everybody," said Blundell, faintly. "Good-bye, Venia. Good-bye, Mr. Turnbull."

"Where's that barrel?" demanded the stout fisher-man, crisply. "Going to be all night with it? Now, two of you—"

Mr. Blundell, with a great effort, and assisted by Venia and the sergeant, sat up. He felt that he had made a good impression, and had no desire to spoil it by riding the barrel. With one exception, everybody was regarding him with moist-eyed admiration. The exception's eyes were, perhaps, the moistest of them all, but admiration had no place in them.

"You're all being made fools of," he said, getting up and stamping. "I tell you he pushed me overboard for the purpose."

"Oh, father! how can you?" demanded Venia, angrily. "He saved your life."

"He pushed me in," repeated the farmer. "Told me to look at a jelly-fish and pushed me in."

"What for?" inquired Sergeant Daly.

"Because—" said Mr. Turnbull. He looked at the unconscious sergeant, and the words on his lips died away in an inarticulate growl.

"What for?" pursued the sergeant, in triumph. "Be reasonable, Mr. Turnbull. Where's the reason in pushing you overboard and then nearly losing his life saving you? That would be a fool's trick. It was as fine a thing as ever I saw."

"What you 'ad, Mr. Turnbull," said the stout fisherman, tapping him on the arm, "was a little touch o' the sun."

"What felt to you like a push," said another man, "and over you went."

"As easy as easy," said a third.

"You're red in the face now," said the stout fisherman, regarding him critically, "and your eyes are starting. You take my advice and get 'ome and get to bed, and the first thing you'll do when you get your senses back will be to go round and thank Mr. Blundell for all 'e's done for you."

Mr. Turnbull looked at them, and the circle of intelligent faces grew misty before his angry eyes. One man, ignoring his sodden condition, recommended a wet handkerchief tied round his brow.

"I don't want any thanks, Mr. Turnbull," said Blundell, feebly, as he was assisted to his feet. "I'd do as much for you again."

The stout fisherman patted him admiringly on the back, and Mr. Turnbull felt like a prophet beholding a realised vision as the spectators clustered round Mr. Blundell and followed their friends' example. Tenderly but firmly they led the hero in triumph up the quay toward home, shouting out eulogistic descriptions of his valour to curious neighbours as they passed. Mr. Turnbull, churlishly keeping his distance in the rear of the procession, received in grim silence the congratulations of his friends.

The extraordinary hallucination caused by the sun-stroke lasted with him for over a week, but at the end of that time his mind cleared and he saw things in the same light as reasonable folk. Venia was the first to congratulate him upon his recovery; but his extraordinary behaviour in proposing to Miss Sippet the very day on which she herself became Mrs. Blundell convinced her that his recovery was only partial.

THE BOATSWAIN'S WATCH

Captain Polson sat in his comfortable parlour smiling benignly upon his daughter and sister. His ship, after an absence of eighteen months, was once more berthed in the small harbour of Barborough, and the captain was sitting in that state of good-natured affability which invariably characterised his first appearance after a long absence.

"No news this end, I suppose," he inquired, after a lengthy recital of most extraordinarily uninteresting adventures.

"Not much," said his sister Jane, looking nervously at her niece. "Young Metcalfe has gone into partnership with his father."

"I don't want to hear about those sharks," said the captain, waxing red. "Tell me about honest men."

"Joe Lewis has had a month's imprisonment for stealing fowls," said Miss Polson meekly. "Mrs. Purton has had twins—dear little fellows they are, fat as butter!—she has named one of them Polson, after you. The greedy one."

"Any deaths?" inquired the captain snappishly, as he eyed the innocent lady suspiciously.

"Poor old Jasper Wheeler has gone," said his sister; "he was very resigned. He borrowed enough money to get a big doctor from London, and when he heard that there was no hope for him he said he was just longing to go, and he was sorry he couldn't take all his dear ones with him. Mary Hewson is married to Jack Draper, and young Metcalfe's banns go up for the third time next Sunday."

"I hope he gets a Tartar," said the vindictive captain. "Who's the girl? Some silly little fool, I know. She ought to be warned!"

"I don't believe in interfering in marriages," said his daughter Chrissie, shaking her head sagely.

"Oh!" said the captain, staring, "YOU don't! Now you've put your hair up and taken to wearing long frocks, I suppose you're beginning to think of it."

"Yes; auntie wants to tell you something!" said his daughter, rising and crossing the room.

"No, I don't!" said Miss Polson hastily.

"You'd better do it," said Chrissie, giving her a little push, "there's a dear; I'll go upstairs and lock myself in my room."

The face of the captain, whilst this conversation was passing, was a study in suppressed emotions. He was a firm advocate for importing the manners of the quarter-deck into private life, the only drawback being that he had to leave behind him the language usual in that locality. To this omission he usually ascribed his failures.

"Sit down, Chrissie," he commanded; "sit down, Jane. Now, miss, what's all this about?"

"I don't like to tell you," said Chrissie, folding her hands in her lap. "I know you'll be cross. You're so unreasonable."

The captain stared—frightfully.

"I'm going to be married," said Chrissie suddenly,—"there! To Jack Metcalfe—there! So you'll have to learn to love him. He's going to try and love you for my sake." To his sister's dismay the captain got up, and brandishing his fists walked violently to and fro. By these simple but unusual means decorum was preserved.

"If you were only a boy," said the captain, when he had regained his seat, "I should know what to do with you."

"If I were a boy," said Chrissie, who, having braced herself up for the fray, meant to go through with it, "I shouldn't want to marry Jack. Don't be silly, father!"

"Jane," said the captain, in a voice which made the lady addressed start in her chair, "what do you mean by it?"

"It isn't my fault," said Miss Polson feebly. "I told her how it would be. And it was so gradual; he admired my geraniums at first, and, of course, I was deceived. There are so many people admire my geraniums; whether it is because the window has a south aspect."

"Oh!" said the captain rudely, "that'll do, Jane. If he wasn't a lawyer, I'd go round and break his neck. Chrissie is only nineteen, and she'll come for a year's cruise with me. Perhaps the sea air'll strengthen her head. We'll see who's master in this family."

"I'm sure I don't want to be master," said his daughter, taking a weapon of fine cambric out of her pocket, and getting ready for action. "I can't help liking people. Auntie likes him too, don't you, auntie?"

"Yes," said Miss Polson bravely.

"Very good," said the autocrat promptly, "I'll take you both for a cruise."

"You're making me very un—unhappy," said Chrissie, burying her face in her handkerchief.

"You'll be more unhappy before I've done with you," said the captain grimly. "And while I think of it, I'll step round and stop those banns." His daughter caught him by the arm as he was passing, and laid her face on his sleeve. "You'll make me look so foolish," she wailed.

"That'll make it easier for you to come to sea with me," said her father. "Don't cry all over my sleeve. I'm going to see a parson. Run upstairs and play with your dolls, and if you're a good girl, I'll bring you in some sweets." He put on his hat, and closing the front door with a bang, went off to the new rector to knock two years off the age which his daughter kept for purposes of matrimony. The rector, grieved at such duplicity in one so young, met him more than half way, and he came out from him smiling placidly, until his attention was attracted by a young man on the other side of the road, who was regarding him with manifest awkwardness.

"Good evening, Captain Polson," he said, crossing the road.

"Oh," said the captain, stopping, "I wanted to speak to you. I suppose you wanted to marry my daughter while I was out of the way, to save trouble. Just the manly thing I should have expected of you. I've stopped the banns, and I'm going to take her for a voyage with me. You'll have to look elsewhere, my lad."

"The ill feeling is all on your side, captain," said Metcalfe, reddening.

"Ill feeling!" snorted the captain. "You put me in the witness-box, and made me a laughing-stock in the place with your silly attempts at jokes, lost me five hundred pounds, and then try and marry my daughter while I'm at sea. Ill feeling be hanged!"

"That was business," said the other.

"It was," said the captain, "and this is business too. Mine. I'll look after it, I'll promise you. I think I know who'll look silly this time. I'd sooner see my girl in heaven than married to a rascal of a lawyer."

"You'd want good glasses," retorted Metcalfe, who was becoming ruffled.

"I don't want to bandy words with you," said the captain with dignity, after a long pause, devoted to thinking of something worth bandying. "You think you're a clever fellow, but I know a cleverer. You're quite welcome to marry my daughter—if you can."

He turned on his heel, and refusing to listen to any further remarks, went on his way rejoicing. Arrived home, he lit his pipe, and throwing himself into an armchair, related his exploits. Chrissie had recourse to her handkerchief again, more for effect than use, but Miss Polson, who was a tender soul, took hers out and wept unrestrainedly. At first the captain took it well enough. It was a tribute to his power, but when they took to sobbing one against the other, his temper rose, and he sternly commanded silence.

"I shall be like—this—every day at sea," sobbed Chrissie vindictively, "only worse; making us all ridiculous."

"Stop that noise directly!" vociferated the captain.

"We c-c-can't," sobbed Miss Polson.

"And we d-don't want to," said Chrissie. "It's all we can do, and we're going to do it. You'd better g-go out and stop something else. You can't stop us."

The captain took the advice and went, and in the billiard-room of the "George" heard some news which set him thinking, and which brought him back somewhat earlier than he had at first intended. A small group at his gate broke up into its elements at his approach, and the captain, following his sister and daughter into the room, sat down and eyed them severely.

"So you're going to run off to London to get married, are you, miss?" he said ferociously. "Well, we'll see. You don't go out of my sight until we sail, and if I catch that pettifogging lawyer round at my gate again, I'll break every bone in his body, mind that."

For the next three days the captain kept his daughter under observation, and never allowed her to stir abroad except in his company. The evening of the third day, to his own great surprise, he spent at a Dorcas. The company was not congenial, several of the ladies putting their work away, and glaring frigidly at the intruder; and though they could see clearly that he was suffering greatly, made no attempt to put him at his ease. He was very thoughtful all the way home, and the next day took a partner into the concern, in the shape of his boatswain.

"You understand, Tucker," he concluded, as the hapless seaman stood in a cringing attitude before Chrissie, "that you never let my daughter out of your sight. When she goes out you go with her."

"Yessir," said Tucker; "and suppose she tells me to go home, what am I to do then?"

"You're a fool," said the captain sharply. "It doesn't matter what she says or does; unless you are in the same room, you are never to be more than three yards from her."

"Make it four, cap'n," said the boatswain, in a broken voice.

"Three," said the captain; "and mind, she's artful. All girls are, and she'll try and give you the slip. I've had information given me as to what's going on. Whatever happens, you are not to leave her."

"I wish you'd get somebody else, sir," said Tucker, very respectfully. "There's a lot of chaps aboard that'd like the job."

"You're the only man I can trust," said the captain shortly. "When I give you orders I know they'll be obeyed; it's your watch now."

He went out humming. Chrissie took up a book and sat down, utterly ignoring the woebegone figure which stood the regulation three yards from her, twisting its cap in its hands.

"I hope, miss," said the boatswain, after standing patiently for three-quarters of an hour, "as 'ow you won't think I sought arter this 'ere little job."

"No," said Chrissie, without looking up.

"I'm just obeying orders," continued the boatswain. "I always git let in for these 'ere little jobs, somehow. The monkeys I've had to look arter aboard ship would frighten you. There never was a monkey on the Monarch but what I was in charge of. That's what a man gets through being trustworthy."

"Just so," said Chrissie, putting down her book. "Well, I'm going into the kitchen now; come along, nursie."

"'Ere, I say, miss!" remonstrated Tucker, flushing.

"I don't know how Susan will like you going in her kitchen," said Chrissie thoughtfully; "however, that's your business."

The unfortunate seaman followed his fair charge into the kitchen, and, leaning against the door-post, doubled up like a limp rag before the terrible glance of its mistress.

"Ho!" said Susan, who took the state of affairs as an insult to the sex in general; "and what might you be wanting?"

"Cap'n's orders," murmured Tucker feebly.

"I'm captain here," said Susan, confronting him with her bare arms akimbo.

"And credit it does you," said the boatswain, looking round admiringly.

"Is it your wish, Miss Chrissie, that this image comes and stalks into my kitchen as if the place belongs to him?" demanded the irate Susan.

"I didn't mean to come in in that way," said the astonished Tucker. "I can't help being big."

"I don't want him here," said her mistress; "what do you think I want him for?"

"You hear that?" said Susan, pointing to the door; "now go. I don't want people to say that you come into this kitchen after me."

"I'm here by the cap'n's orders," said Tucker faintly. "I don't want to be here—far from it. As for people saying that I come here after you, them as knows me would laugh at the idea."

"If I had my way," said Susan, in a hard rasping voice, "I'd box your ears for you. That's what I'd do to you, and you can go and tell the cap'n I said so. Spy!"

This was the first verse of the first watch, and there were many verses. To add to his discomfort he was confined to the house, as his charge manifested no desire to go outside, and as neither she nor her aunt cared about the trouble of bringing him to a fit and proper state of subjection, the task became a labour of love for the energetic Susan. In spite of everything, however, he stuck to his guns, and the indignant Chrissie, who was in almost hourly communication with Metcalfe through the medium of her faithful handmaiden, was rapidly becoming desperate.

On the fourth day, time getting short, Chrissie went on a new tack with her keeper, and Susan, sorely against her will, had to follow suit. Chrissie smiled at him, Susan called him Mr. Tucker, and Miss Polson gave him a glass of her best wine. From the position of an outcast, he jumped in one bound to that of confidential adviser. Miss Polson told him many items of family interest, and later on in the afternoon actually consulted him as to a bad cold which Chrissie had developed.

He prescribed half-a-pint of linseed oil hot, but Miss Polson favoured chlorodyne. The conversation then turned on the deadly qualities of that drug when taken in excess, of the fatal sleep in which it lulled its victims. So disastrous were the incidents cited, that half an hour later, when, her aunt and Susan being out, Chrissie took a small bottle of chlorodyne from the mantel-piece, the boatswain implored her to try his nastier but safer remedy instead.

"Nonsense!" said Chrissie, "I'm only going to take twenty drops—one—two—three—"

The drug suddenly poured out in a little stream.

"I should think that's about it," said Chrissie, holding the tumbler up to the light.

"It's about five hundred!" said the horrified Tucker. "Don't take that, miss, whatever you do; let me measure it for you."

The girl waved him away, and, before he could interfere, drank off the contents of the glass and resumed her seat. The boatswain watched her uneasily, and taking up the phial carefully read through the directions. After that he was not at all surprised to see the book fall from his charge's hand on to the floor, and her eyes close.

"I knowed it," said Tucker, in a profuse perspiration, "I knowed it. Them blamed gals are all alike. Always knows what's best. Miss Polson! Miss Polson!"

He shook her roughly, but to no purpose, and then running to the door, shouted eagerly for Susan. No reply forthcoming he ran to the window, but there was nobody in sight, and he came back and stood in front of the girl, wringing his huge hands helplessly. It was a great question for a poor sailor-man. If he went for the doctor he deserted his post; if he didn't go his charge might die. He made one more attempt to awaken her, and, seizing a flower-glass, splashed her freely with cold water. She did not even wince.

"It's no use fooling with it," murmured Tucker; "I must get the doctor, that's all."

He quitted the room, and, dashing hastily downstairs, had already opened the hall door when a thought struck him, and he came back again. Chrissie was still asleep in the chair, and, with a smile at the clever way in which he had solved a difficulty, he stooped down, and, raising her in his strong arms, bore her from the room and downstairs. Then a hitch occurred. The triumphant progress was marred by the behaviour of the hall door, which, despite his efforts, refused to be opened, and, encumbered by his fair burden, he could not for some time ascertain the reason. Then, full of shame that so much deceit could exist in so fair and frail a habitation, he discovered that Miss Polson's foot was pressing firmly against it. Her eyes were still closed and her head heavy, but the fact remained that one foot was acting in a manner that was full of intelligence and guile, and when he took it away from the door the other one took its place. By a sudden manoeuvre the wily Tucker turned his back on the door, and opened it, and, at the same moment, a hand came to life again and dealt him a stinging slap on the face.

"Idiot!" said the indignant Chrissie, slipping from his arms and confronting him. "How dare you take such a liberty?"

The astonished boatswain felt his face, and regarded her open-mouthed.

"Don't you ever dare to speak to me again," said the offended maiden, drawing herself up with irreproachable dignity. "I am disgusted with your conduct. Most unbearable!"

"I was carrying you off to the doctor," said the boatswain." How was I to know you was only shamming?"

"SHAMMING?" said Chrissie, in tones of incredulous horror. "I was asleep. I often go to sleep in the afternoon."

The boatswain made no reply, except to grin with great intelligence as he followed his charge upstairs again. He grinned at intervals until the return of Susan and Miss Polson, who, trying to look unconcerned, came in later on, both apparently suffering from temper, Susan especially. Amid the sympathetic interruptions of these listeners Chrissie recounted her experiences, while the boatswain, despite his better sense, felt like the greatest scoundrel unhung, a feeling which was fostered by the remarks of Susan and the chilling regards of Miss Poison.

"I shall inform the captain," said Miss Polson, bridling. "It's my duty."

"Oh, I shall tell him," said Chrissie. "I shall tell him the moment he comes in at the door."

"So shall I," said Susan; "the idea of taking such liberties!"

Having fired this broadside, the trio watched the enemy narrowly and anxiously.

"If I've done anything wrong, ladies," said the unhappy boatswain, "I am sorry for it. I can't say anything fairer than that, and I'll tell the cap'n myself exactly how I came to do it when he comes in."

"Pah! tell-tale!" said Susan.

"Of course, if you are here to fetch and carry," said Miss Polson, with withering emphasis.

"The idea of a grown man telling tales," said Chrissie scornfully. "Baby!"

"Why, just now you were all going to tell him yourselves," said the bewildered boatswain.

The two elder women rose and regarded him with looks of pitying disdain. Miss Polson's glance said "Fool!' plainly; Susan, a simple child of nature, given to expressing her mind freely, said "Blockhead!" with conviction.

"I see 'ow it is," said the boatswain, after ruminating deeply. "Well, I won't split, ladies. I can see now you was all in it, and it was a little job to get me out of the house."

"What a head he has got," said the irritated Susan; "isn't it wonderful how he thinks of it all! Nobody would think he was so clever to look at him."

"Still waters run deep," said the boatswain, who was beginning to have a high opinion of himself.

"And pride goes before a fall," said Chrissie; "remember that, Mr. Tucker."

Mr. Tucker grinned, but, remembering the fable of the pitcher and the well, pressed his superior officer that evening to relieve him from his duties. He stated that the strain was slowly undermining a constitution which was not so strong as appearances would warrant, and that his knowledge of female nature was lamentably deficient on many important points. "You're doing very well," said the captain, who had no intention of attending any more Dorcases, "very well indeed; I am proud of you."

"It isn't a man's work," objected the boatswain. "Besides, if anything happens you'll blame me for it."

"Nothing can happen," declared the captain confidently. "We shall make a start in about four days now. You're the only man I can trust with such a difficult job, Tucker, and I shan't forget you,"

"Very good," said the other dejectedly. "I obey orders, then."

The next day passed quietly, the members of the household making a great fuss of Tucker, and thereby filling him with forebodings of the worst possible nature. On the day after, when the captain, having business at a neighbouring town, left him in sole charge, his uneasiness could not be concealed.

"I'm going for a walk," said Chrissie, as he sat by himself, working out dangerous moves and the best means of checking them; "would you care to come with me, Tucker?"

"I wish you wouldn't put it that way, miss," said the boatswain, as he reached for his hat.

"I want exercise," said Chrissie; "I've been cooped up long enough."

She set off at a good pace up the High Street, attended by her faithful follower, and passing through the small suburbs, struck out into the country beyond. After four miles the boatswain, who was no walker, reminded her that they had got to go back.

"Plenty of time," said Chrissie, "we have got the day before us. Isn't it glorious? Do you see that milestone, Tucker? I'll race you to it; come along."

She was off on the instant, with the boatswain, who suspected treachery, after her.

"You CAN run," she panted, thoughtfully, as she came in second; "we'll have another one presently. You don't know how good it is for you, Tucker."

The boatswain grinned sourly and looked at her from the corner of his eye. The next three miles passed like a horrible nightmare; his charge making a race for every milestone, in which the labouring boatswain, despite his want of practice, came in the winner. The fourth ended disastrously, Chrissie limping the last ten yards, and seating herself with a very woebegone face on the stone itself.

"You did very well, miss," said the boatswain, who thought he could afford to be generous. "You needn't be offended about it."

"It's my ankle," said Chrissie with a little whimper. "Oh! I twisted it right round."

The boatswain stood regarding her in silent consternation

"It's no use looking like that," said Chrissie sharply, "you great clumsy thing. If you hadn't have run so hard it wouldn't have happened. It's all your fault."

"If you don't mind leaning on me a bit," said Tucker, "we might get along."

Chrissie took his arm petulantly, and they started on their return journey, at the rate of about four hours a mile, with little cries and gasps at every other yard.

"It's no use," said Chrissie as she relinquished his arm, and, limping to the side of the road, sat down. The boatswain pricked up his ears hopefully at the sound of approaching wheels.

"What's the matter with the young lady?" inquired a groom who was driving a little trap, as he pulled up and regarded with interest a grimace of extraordinary intensity on the young lady's face.

"Broke her ankle, I think," said the boatswain glibly. "Which way are you going?"

"Well, I'm going to Barborough," said the groom; "but my guvnor's rather pertickler."

"I'll make it all right with you," said the boatswain.

The groom hesitated a minute, and then made way for Chrissie as the boatswain assisted her to get up beside him; then Tucker, with a grin of satisfaction at getting a seat once more, clambered up behind, and they started.

"Have a rug, mate," said the groom, handing the reins to Chrissie and passing it over; "put it round your knees and tuck the ends under you."

"Ay, ay, mate," said the boatswain as he obeyed the instructions.

"Are you sure you are quite comfortable?" said the groom affectionately.

"Quite," said the other.

The groom said no more, but in a quiet business-like fashion placed his hands on the seaman's broad back, and shot him out into the road. Then he snatched up the reins and drove off at a gallop.

Without the faintest hope of winning, Mr. Tucker, who realised clearly, appearances notwithstanding, that he had fallen into a trap, rose after a hurried rest and started on his fifth race that morning. The prize was only a second-rate groom with plated buttons, who was waving cheery farewells to him with a dingy top hat; but the boatswain would have sooner had it than a silver tea-service.

He ran as he had never ran before in his life, but all to no purpose, the trap stopping calmly a little further on to take up another passenger, in whose favour the groom retired to the back seat; then, with a final wave of the hand to him, they took a road to the left and drove rapidly out of sight. The boatswain's watch was over.

THE BOATSWAIN'S MATE

Mr. George Benn, retired boat-swain, sighed noisily, and with a despondent gesture, turned to the door and stood with the handle in his hand; Mrs. Waters, sitting behind the tiny bar in a tall Windsor-chair, eyed him with some heat.

"My feelings'll never change," said the boatswain.

"Nor mine either," said the landlady, sharply. "It's a strange thing, Mr. Benn, but you always ask me to marry you after the third mug."

"It's only to get my courage up," pleaded the boatswain. "Next time I'll do it afore I 'ave a drop; that'll prove to you I'm in earnest."

He stepped outside and closed the door before the landlady could make a selection from the many retorts that crowded to her lips.

After the cool bar, with its smell of damp saw-dust, the road seemed hot and dusty; but the boatswain, a prey to gloom natural to a man whose hand has been refused five times in a fortnight, walked on unheeding. His steps lagged, but his brain was active.

He walked for two miles deep in thought, and then coming to a shady bank took a seat upon an inviting piece of turf and lit his pipe. The heat and the drowsy hum of bees made him nod; his pipe hung from the corner of his mouth, and his eyes closed.

He opened them at the sound of approaching footsteps, and, feeling in his pocket for matches, gazed lazily at the intruder. He saw a tall man carrying a small bundle over his shoulder, and in the erect carriage, the keen eyes, and bronzed face had little difficulty in detecting the old soldier.

The stranger stopped as he reached the seated boatswain and eyed him pleasantly.

"Got a pipe o' baccy, mate?" he inquired.

The boatswain handed him the small metal box in which he kept that luxury.

"Lobster, ain't you?" he said, affably.

The tall man nodded. "Was," he replied. "Now I'm my own commander-in-chief."

"Padding it?" suggested the boatswain, taking the box from him and refilling his pipe.

The other nodded, and with the air of one disposed to conversation dropped his bundle in the ditch and took a seat beside him. "I've got plenty of time," he remarked.

Mr. Benn nodded, and for a while smoked on in silence. A dim idea which had been in his mind for some time began to clarify. He stole a glance at his companion—a man of about thirty-eight, clear eyes, with humorous wrinkles at the corners, a heavy moustache, and a cheerful expression more than tinged with recklessness.

"Ain't over and above fond o' work?" suggested the boatswain, when he had finished his inspection.

"I love it," said the other, blowing a cloud of smoke in the air, "but we can't have all we want in this world; it wouldn't be good for us."

The boatswain thought of Mrs. Waters, and sighed. Then he rattled his pocket.

"Would arf a quid be any good to you?" he inquired.

"Look here," began the soldier; "just because I asked you for a pipe o' baccy—"

"No offence," said the other, quickly. "I mean if you earned it?"

The soldier nodded and took his pipe from his mouth. "Gardening and windows?" he hazarded, with a shrug of his shoulders.

The boatswain shook his head.

"Scrubbing, p'r'aps?" said the soldier, with a sigh of resignation. "Last house I scrubbed out I did it so thoroughly they accused me of pouching the soap. Hang 'em!"

"And you didn't?" queried the boatswain, eyeing him keenly.

The soldier rose and, knocking the ashes out of his pipe, gazed at him darkly. "I can't give it back to you," he said, slowly, "because I've smoked some of it, and I can't pay you for it because I've only got twopence, and that I want for myself. So long, matey, and next time a poor wretch asks you for a pipe, be civil."

"I never see such a man for taking offence in all my born days," expostulated the boat-swain. "I 'ad my reasons for that remark, mate. Good reasons they was."

The soldier grunted and, stooping, picked up his bundle.

"I spoke of arf a sovereign just now," continued the boatswain, impressively, "and when I tell you that I offer it to you to do a bit o' burgling, you'll see 'ow necessary it is for me to be certain of your honesty."

"*Burgling?*" gasped the astonished soldier. "*Honesty?* 'Struth; are you drunk or am I?"

"Meaning," said the boatswain, waving the imputation away with his hand, "for you to pretend to be a burglar."

"We're both drunk, that's what it is," said the other, resignedly.

The boatswain fidgeted. "If you don't agree, mum's the word and no 'arm done," he said, holding out his hand.

"Mum's the word," said the soldier, taking it. "My name's Ned Travers, and, barring cells for a spree now and again, there's nothing against it. Mind that."

"Might 'appen to anybody," said Mr. Benn, soothingly. "You fill your pipe and don't go chucking good tobacco away agin."

Mr. Travers took the offered box and, with economy born of adversity, stooped and filled up first with the plug he had thrown away. Then he resumed his seat and, leaning back luxuriously, bade the other "fire away."

"I ain't got it all ship-shape and proper yet," said Mr. Benn, slowly, "but it's in my mind's eye. It's been there off and on like for some time."

He lit his pipe again and gazed fixedly at the opposite hedge. "Two miles from here, where I live," he said, after several vigorous puffs, "there's a little public-'ouse called the Beehive, kept by a lady wot I've got my eye on."

The soldier sat up.

"She won't 'ave me," said the boatswain, with an air of mild surprise.

The soldier leaned back again.

"She's a lone widder," continued Mr. Benn, shaking his head, "and the Beehive is in a lonely place. It's right through the village, and the nearest house is arf a mile off."

"Silly place for a pub," commented Mr. Travers.

"I've been telling her 'ow unsafe it is," said the boatswain. "I've been telling her that she wants a man to protect her, and she only laughs at me. She don't believe it; d'ye see? Likewise I'm a small man—small, but stiff. She likes tall men."

"Most women do," said Mr. Travers, sitting upright and instinctively twisting his moustache. "When I was in the ranks—"

"My idea is," continued the boatswain, slightly raising his voice, "to kill two birds with one stone—prove to her that she does want being protected, and that I'm the man to protect her. D'ye take my meaning, mate?"

The soldier reached out a hand and felt the other's biceps. "Like a lump o' wood," he said, approvingly.

"My opinion is," said the boatswain, with a faint smirk, "that she loves me without knowing it."

"They often do," said Mr. Travers, with a grave shake of his head.

"Consequently I don't want 'er to be disappointed," said the other.

"It does you credit," remarked Mr. Travers.

"I've got a good head," said Mr. Benn, "else I shouldn't 'ave got my rating as boatswain as soon as I did; and I've been turning it over in my mind, over and over agin, till my brain-pan fair aches with it. Now, if you do what I want you to to-night and it comes off all right, damme I'll make it a quid."

"Go on, Vanderbilt," said Mr. Travers; "I'm listening."

The boatswain gazed at him fixedly. "You meet me 'ere in this spot at eleven o'clock to-night," he said, solemnly; "and I'll take you to her 'ouse and put you through a little winder I know of. You goes upstairs and alarms her, and she screams for help. I'm watching the house, faithful-like, and hear 'er scream. I dashes in at the winder, knocks you down, and rescues her. D'ye see?"

"I hear," corrected Mr. Travers, coldly.

"She clings to me," continued the boat-swain, with a rapt expression of face, "in her gratitood, and, proud of my strength and pluck, she marries me."

"An' I get a five years' honeymoon," said the soldier.

The boatswain shook his head and patted the other's shoulder. "In the excitement of the moment you spring up and escape," he said, with a kindly smile. "I've thought it all out. You can run much faster than I can; any-ways, you will. The nearest 'ouse is arf a mile off, as I said, and her servant is staying till to-morrow at 'er mother's, ten miles away."

Mr. Travers rose to his feet and stretched himself. "Time I was toddling," he said, with a yawn. "Thanks for amusing me, mate."

"You won't do it?" said the boatswain, eyeing him with much concern.

"I'm hanged if I do," said the soldier, emphatically. "Accidents will happen, and then where should I be?"

"If they did," said the boatswain, "I'd own up and clear you."

"You might," said Mr. Travers, "and then again you mightn't. So long, mate."

"I—I'll make it two quid," said the boat-swain, trembling with eagerness. "I've took a fancy to you; you're just the man for the job."

The soldier, adjusting his bundle, glanced at him over his shoulder. "Thankee," he said, with mock gratitude.

"Look 'ere," said the boatswain, springing up and catching him by the sleeve; "I'll give it to you in writing. Come, you ain't faint-hearted? Why, a bluejacket 'ud do it for the fun o' the thing. If I give it to you in writing, and there should be an accident, it's worse for me than it is for you, ain't it?"

Mr. Travers hesitated and, pushing his cap back, scratched his head.

"I gives you the two quid afore you go into the house," continued the boatswain, hastily following up the impression he had made. "I'd give 'em to you now if I'd got 'em with me. That's my confidence in you; I likes the look of you. Soldier or sailor, when there is a man's work to be done, give 'em to me afore anybody."

The soldier seated himself again and let his bundle fall to the ground. "Go on," he said, slowly. "Write it out fair and square and sign it, and I'm your man."

The boatswain clapped him on the shoulder and produced a bundle of papers from his pocket. "There's letters there with my name and address on 'em," he said. "It's all fair, square, and above-board. When you've cast your eyes over them I'll give you the writing."

Mr. Travers took them and, re-lighting his pipe, smoked in silence, with various side glances at his companion as that enthusiast sucked his pencil and sat twisting in the agonies of composition. The document finished—after several failures had been retrieved and burnt by the careful Mr. Travers—the boat-swain heaved a sigh of relief, and handing it over to him, leaned back with a complacent air while he read it.

"Seems all right," said the soldier, folding it up and putting it in his waistcoat-pocket. "I'll be here at eleven to-night."

"Eleven it is," said the boatswain, briskly, "and, between pals—here's arf a dollar to go on with."

He patted him on the shoulder again, and with a caution to keep out of sight as much as possible till night walked slowly home. His step was light, but he carried a face in which care and exultation were strangely mingled.

By ten o'clock that night care was in the ascendant, and by eleven, when he discerned the red glow of Mr. Travers's pipe set as a beacon against a dark background of hedge, the boatswain was ready to curse his inventive powers. Mr. Travers greeted him cheerily and, honestly attributing the fact to good food and a couple of pints of beer he had had since the boatswain left him, said that he was ready for anything.

Mr. Benn grunted and led the way in silence. There was no moon, but the night was clear, and Mr. Travers, after one or two light-hearted attempts at conversation, abandoned the effort and fell to whistling softly instead.

Except for one lighted window the village slept in darkness, but the boatswain, who had been walking with the stealth of a Red Indian on the war-path, breathed more freely after they had left it behind. A renewal of his antics a little farther on apprised Mr. Travers that they were approaching their destination, and a minute or two later they came to a small inn standing just off the road. "All shut up and Mrs. Waters abed, bless her," whispered the boatswain, after walking care-fully round the house. "How do you feel?"

"I'm all right," said Mr. Travers. "I feel as if I'd been burgling all my life. How do you feel?"

"Narvous," said Mr. Benn, pausing under a small window at the rear of the house. "This is the one."

Mr. Travers stepped back a few paces and gazed up at the house. All was still. For a few moments he stood listening and then re-joined the boatswain.

"Good-bye, mate," he said, hoisting himself on to the sill. "Death or victory."

The boatswain whispered and thrust a couple of sovereigns into his hand. "Take your time; there's no hurry," he muttered. "I want to pull myself together. Frighten 'er enough, but not too much. When she screams I'll come in."

Mr. Travers slipped inside and then thrust his head out of the window. "Won't she think it funny you should be so handy?" he inquired.

"No; it's my faithful 'art," said the boat-swain, "keeping watch over her every night, that's the ticket. She won't know no better."

Mr. Travers grinned, and removing his boots passed them out to the other. "We don't want her to hear me till I'm upstairs," he whispered. "Put 'em outside, handy for me to pick up."

The boatswain obeyed, and Mr. Travers—who was by no means a good hand at darning socks—shivered as he trod lightly over a stone floor. Then, following the instructions of Mr. Benn, he made his way to the stairs and mounted noiselessly.

But for a slight stumble half-way up his progress was very creditable for an amateur. He paused and listened and, all being silent, made his way to the landing and stopped out-side a door. Despite himself his heart was beating faster than usual.

He pushed the door open slowly and started as it creaked. Nothing happening he pushed again, and standing just inside saw, by a small ewer silhouetted against the casement, that he was in a bedroom. He listened for the sound of breathing, but in vain.

"Quiet sleeper," he reflected; "or perhaps it is an empty room. Now, I wonder whether—"

The sound of an opening door made him start violently, and he stood still, scarcely breathing, with his ears on the alert. A light shone on the landing, and peeping round the door he saw a woman coming along the corridor—a younger and better-looking woman than he had expected to see. In one hand she held aloft a candle, in the other she bore a double-barrelled gun. Mr. Travers withdrew into the room and, as the light came nearer, slipped into a big cupboard by the side of the fireplace and, standing bolt upright, waited. The light came into the room.

"Must have been my fancy," said a pleasant voice.

"Bless her," smiled Mr. Travers.

His trained ear recognized the sound of cocking triggers. The next moment a heavy body bumped against the door of the cupboard and the key turned in the lock.

"Got you!" said the voice, triumphantly. "Keep still; if you try and break out I shall shoot you."

"All right," said Mr. Travers, hastily; "I won't move."

"Better not," said the voice. "Mind, I've got a gun pointing straight at you."

"Point it downwards, there's a good girl," said Mr. Travers, earnestly; "and take your finger off the trigger. If anything happened to me you'd never forgive yourself."

"It's all right so long as you don't move," said the voice; "and I'm not a girl," it added, sternly.

"Yes, you are," said the prisoner. "I saw you. I thought it was an angel at first. I saw your little bare feet and—"

A faint scream interrupted him.

"You'll catch cold," urged Mr. Travers.

"Don't you trouble about me," said the voice, tartly.

"I won't give any trouble," said Mr. Travers, who began to think it was time for the boatswain to appear on the scene. "Why don't you call for help? I'll go like a lamb."

"I don't want your advice," was the reply. "I know what to do. Now, don't you try and break out. I'm going to fire one barrel out of the window, but I've got the other one for you if you move."

"My dear girl," protested the horrified Mr. Travers, "you'll alarm the neighbourhood."

"Just what I want to do," said the voice. "Keep still, mind."

Mr. Travers hesitated. The game was up, and it was clear that in any case the stratagem of the ingenious Mr. Benn would have to be disclosed.

"Stop!" he said, earnestly. "Don't do anything rash. I'm not a burglar; I'm doing this for a friend of yours—Mr. Benn."

"What?" said an amazed voice.

"True as I stand here," asseverated Mr. Travers. "Here, here's my instructions. I'll put 'em under the door, and if you go to the back window you'll see him in the garden waiting."

He rustled the paper under the door, and it was at once snatched from his fingers. He regained an upright position and stood listening to the startled and indignant exclamations of his gaoler as she read the boatswain's permit:

"Sound mind—above-board—ship-shape," repeated a dazed voice. "Where is he?"

"Out at the back," replied Mr. Travers. "If you go to the window you can see him. Now, do put something round your shoulders, there's a good girl."

There was no reply, but a board creaked. He waited for what seemed a long time, and then the board creaked again.

"Did you see him?" he inquired.

"I did," was the sharp reply. "You both ought to be ashamed of yourselves. You ought to be punished."

"There is a clothes-peg sticking into the back of my head," remarked Mr. Travers. "What are you going to do?"

There was no reply.

"What are you going to do?" repeated Mr. Travers, somewhat uneasily. "You look too nice to do anything hard; leastways, so far as I can judge through this crack."

There was a smothered exclamation, and then sounds of somebody moving hastily about the room and the swish of clothing hastily donned.

"You ought to have done it before," commented the thoughtful Mr. Travers. "It's enough to give you your death of cold."

"Mind your business," said the voice, sharply. "Now, if I let you out, will you promise to do exactly as I tell you?"

"Honour bright," said Mr. Travers, fervently.

"I'm going to give Mr. Benn a lesson he won't forget," proceeded the other, grimly. "I'm going to fire off this gun, and then run down and tell him I've killed you."

"Eh?" said the amazed Mr. Travers. "Oh, Lord!"

"H'sh! Stop that laughing," commanded the voice. "He'll hear you. Be quiet!"

The key turned in the lock, and Mr. Travers, stepping forth, clapped his hand over his mouth and endeavoured to obey. Mrs. Waters, stepping back with the gun ready, scrutinized him closely.

"Come on to the landing," said Mr. Travers, eagerly. "We don't want anybody else to hear. Fire into this."

He snatched a patchwork rug from the floor and stuck it up against the balusters. "You stay here," said Mrs. Waters. He nodded.

She pointed the gun at the hearth-rug, the walls shook with the explosion, and, with a shriek that set Mr. Travers's teeth on edge, she rushed downstairs and, drawing back the bolts of the back door, tottered outside and into the arms of the agitated boatswain.

"Oh! oh! oh!" she cried.

"What—what's the matter?" gasped the boatswain.

The widow struggled in his arms. "A burglar," she said, in a tense whisper. "But it's all right; I've killed him."

"Kill—" stuttered the other. "Kill—*Killed him?*"

Mrs. Waters nodded and released herself, "First shot," she said, with a satisfied air.

The boatswain wrung his hands. "Good heavens!" he said, moving slowly towards the door. "Poor fellow!"

"Come back," said the widow, tugging at his coat.

"I was—was going to see—whether I could do anything for 'im," quavered the boatswain. "Poor fellow!"

"You stay where you are," commanded Mrs. Waters. "I don't want any witnesses. I don't want this house to have a bad name. I'm going to keep it quiet."

"Quiet?" said the shaking boatswain. "How?"

"First thing to do," said the widow, thoughtfully, "is to get rid of the body. I'll bury him in the garden, I think. There's a very good bit of ground behind those potatoes. You'll find the spade in the tool-house."

The horrified Mr. Benn stood stock-still regarding her.

"While you're digging the grave," continued Mrs. 'Waters, calmly, "I'll go in and clean up the mess."

The boatswain reeled and then fumbled with trembling fingers at his collar.

Like a man in a dream he stood watching as she ran to the tool-house and returned with a spade and pick; like a man in a dream he followed her on to the garden.

"Be careful," she said, sharply; "you're treading down my potatoes."

The boatswain stopped dead and stared at her. Apparently unconscious of his gaze, she began to pace out the measurements and then, placing the tools in his hands, urged him to lose no time.

"I'll bring him down when you're gone," she said, looking towards the house.

The boatswain wiped his damp brow with the back of his hand. "How are you going to get it downstairs?" he breathed.

"Drag it," said Mrs. Waters, briefly.

"Suppose he isn't dead?" said the boat-swain, with a gleam of hope.

"Fiddlesticks!" said Mrs. Waters. "Do you think I don't know? Now, don't waste time talking; and mind you dig it deep. I'll put a few cabbages on top afterwards—I've got more than I want."

She re-entered the house and ran lightly upstairs. The candle was still alight and the gun was leaning against the bed-post; but the visitor had disappeared. Conscious of an odd feeling of disappointment, she looked round the empty room.

"Come and look at him," entreated a voice, and she turned and beheld the amused countenance of her late prisoner at the door.

"I've been watching from the back window," he said, nodding. "You're a wonder; that's what you are. Come and look at him."

Mrs. Waters followed, and leaning out of the window watched with simple pleasure the efforts of the amateur sexton. Mr. Benn was digging like one possessed, only pausing at intervals to straighten his back and to cast a fearsome glance around him. The only thing that marred her pleasure was the behaviour of Mr. Travers, who was struggling for a place with all the fervour of a citizen at the Lord Mayor's show.

"Get back," she said, in a fierce whisper. "He'll see you."

Mr. Travers with obvious reluctance obeyed, just as the victim looked up.

"Is that you, Mrs. Waters?" inquired the boatswain, fearfully.

"Yes, of course it is," snapped the widow. "Who else should it be, do you think? Go on! What are you stopping for?"

Mr. Benn's breathing as he bent to his task again was distinctly audible. The head of Mr. Travers ranged itself once more alongside the widow's. For a long time they watched in silence.

"Won't you come down here, Mrs. Waters?" called the boatswain, looking up so suddenly that Mr. Travers's head bumped painfully against the side of the window. "It's a bit creepy, all alone."

"I'm all right," said Mrs. Waters.

"I keep fancying there's something dodging behind them currant bushes," pursued the unfortunate Mr. Benn, hoarsely. "How you can stay there alone I can't think. I thought I saw something looking over your shoulder just now. Fancy if it came creeping up behind and caught hold of you! The widow gave a sudden faint scream.

"If you do that again" she said, turning fiercely on Mr. Travers.

"He put it into my head," said the culprit, humbly; "I should never have thought of such a thing by myself. I'm one of the quietest and best-behaved—"

"Make haste, Mr. Benn," said the widow, turning to the window again; "I've got a lot to do when you've finished."

The boatswain groaned and fell to digging again, and Mrs. Waters, after watching a little while longer, gave Mr. Travers some pointed instructions about the window and went down to the garden again.

"That will do, I think," she said, stepping into the hole and regarding it critically. "Now you'd better go straight off home, and, mind, not a word to a soul about this."

She put her hand on his shoulder, and noticing with pleasure that he shuddered at her touch led the way to the gate. The boat-swain paused for a moment, as though about to speak, and then, apparently thinking better of it, bade her good-bye in a hoarse voice and walked feebly up the road. Mrs. Waters stood watching until his steps died away in the distance, and then, returning to the garden, took up the spade and stood regarding with some dismay the mountainous result of his industry. Mr. Travers, who was standing just inside the back door, joined her.

"Let me," he said, gallantly.

The day was breaking as he finished his task. The clean, sweet air and the exercise had given him an appetite to which the smell of cooking bacon and hot coffee that proceeded from the house had set a sharper edge. He took his coat from a bush and put it on. Mrs. Waters appeared at the door.

"You had better come in and have some breakfast before you go," she said, brusquely; "there's no more sleep for me now."

Mr. Travers obeyed with alacrity, and after a satisfying wash in the scullery came into the big kitchen with his face shining and took a seat at the table. The cloth was neatly laid, and Mrs. Waters, fresh and cool, with a smile upon her pleasant face, sat behind the tray. She looked at her guest curiously, Mr. Travers's spirits being somewhat higher than the state of his wardrobe appeared to justify.

"Why don't you get some settled work?" she inquired, with gentle severity, as he imparted snatches of his history between bites.

"Easier said than done," said Mr. Travers, serenely. "But don't you run away with the idea that I'm a beggar, because I'm not. I pay my way, such as it is. And, by-the-bye, I s'pose I haven't earned that two pounds Benn gave me?"

His face lengthened, and he felt uneasily in his pocket.

"I'll give them to him when I'm tired of the joke," said the widow, holding out her hand and watching him closely.

Mr. Travers passed the coins over to her. "Soft hand you've got," he said, musingly. "I don't wonder Benn was desperate. I dare say I should have done the same in his place."

Mrs. Waters bit her lip and looked out at the window; Mr. Travers resumed his breakfast.

"There's only one job that I'm really fit for, now that I'm too old for the Army," he said, confidentially, as, breakfast finished, he stood at the door ready to depart.

"Playing at burglars?" hazarded Mrs. Waters.

"Landlord of a little country public-house," said Mr. Travers, simply.

Mrs. Waters fell back and regarded him with open-eyed amazement.

"Good morning," she said, as soon as she could trust her voice.

"Good-bye," said Mr. Travers, reluctantly. "I should like to hear how old Benn takes this joke, though."

Mrs. Waters retreated into the house and stood regarding him. "If you're passing this way again and like to look in—I'll tell you," she said, after a long pause. "Good-bye."

"I'll look in in a week's time," said Mr. Travers.

He took the proffered hand and shook it warmly. "It would be the best joke of all," he said, turning away.

"What would?"

The soldier confronted her again.

"For old Benn to come round here one evening and find me landlord. Think it over."

Mrs. Waters met his gaze soberly. "I'll think it over when you have gone," she said, softly. "Now go."

BOB'S REDEMPTION

"Gratitoode!" said the night-watchman, with a hard laugh. "*Hmf!* Don't talk to me about gratitoode; I've seen too much of it. If people wot I've helped in my time 'ad only done arf their dooty—arf, mind you—I should be riding in my carriage."

Forgetful of the limitations of soap-boxes he attempted to illustrate his remark by lolling, and nearly went over backwards. Recovering himself by an effort he gazed sternly across the river and smoked fiercely. It was evident that he was brooding over an ill-used past.

'Arry Thomson was one of them, he said, at last. For over six months I wrote all 'is love-letters for him, 'e being an iggernerant sort of man and only being able to do the kisses at the end, which he always insisted on doing 'imself: being jealous. Only three weeks arter he was married 'e come up to where I was standing one day and set about me without saying a word. I was a single man at the time and I didn't understand it. My idea was that he 'ad gone mad, and, being pretty artful and always 'aving a horror of mad people, I let 'im chase me into a police-station. Leastways, I would ha' let 'im, but he didn't come, and I all but got fourteen days for being drunk and disorderly.

Then there was Bill Clark. He 'ad been keeping comp'ny with a gal and got tired of it, and to oblige 'im I went to her and told 'er he was a married man with five children. Bill was as pleased as Punch at fust, but as soon as she took up with another chap he came round to see me and said as I'd ruined his life. We 'ad words about it—naturally—and I did ruin it then to the extent of a couple o' ribs. I went to see 'im in the horsepittle—place I've always been fond of—and the langwidge he used to me was so bad that they sent for the Sister to 'ear it.

That's on'y two out of dozens I could name. Arf the unpleasantnesses in my life 'ave come out of doing kindnesses to people, and all the gratitoode I've 'ad for it I could put in a pint-pot with a pint o' beer already in it.

The only case o' real gratitoode I ever heard of 'appened to a shipmate o' mine—a young chap named Bob Evans. Coming home from Auckland in a barque called the *Dragon Fly* he fell overboard, and another chap named George Crofts, one o' the best swimmers I ever knew, went overboard arter 'im and saved his life.

We was hardly moving at the time, and the sea was like a duck pond, but to 'ear Bob Evans talk you'd ha' thought that George Crofts was the bravest-'arted chap that ever lived. He 'adn't liked him afore, same as the rest of us, George being a sly, mean sort o' chap; but arter George 'ad saved his life 'e couldn't praise 'im enough. He said that so long as he 'ad a crust George should share it, and wotever George asked 'im he should have.

The unfortnit part of it was that George took 'im at his word, and all the rest of the v'y'ge he acted as though Bob belonged to 'im, and by the time we got into the London river Bob couldn't call his soul 'is own. He used to take a room when he was ashore and live very steady, as 'e was saving up to get married, and as soon as he found that out George invited 'imself to stay with him.

"It won't cost you a bit more," he ses, "not if you work it properly."

Bob didn't work it properly, but George having saved his life, and never letting 'im forget it, he didn't like to tell him so. He thought he'd let 'im see gradual that he'd got to be careful because of 'is gal, and the fust evening they was ashore 'e took 'im along with 'im there to tea.

Gerty Mitchell—that was the gal's name—'adn't heard of Bob's accident, and when she did she gave a little scream, and putting 'er arms round his neck, began to kiss 'im right in front of George and her mother.

"You ought to give him one too," ses Mrs. Mitchell, pointing to George.

George wiped 'is mouth on the back of his 'and, but Gerty pretended not to 'ear.

"Fancy if you'd been drownded!" she ses, hugging Bob agin.

"He was pretty near," ses George, shaking his 'ead. "I'm a pore swimmer, but I made up my mind either to save 'im or else go down to a watery grave myself."

He wiped his mouth on the back of his 'and agin, but all the notice Gerty took of it was to send her young brother Ted out for some beer. Then they all 'ad supper together, and Mrs. Mitchell drank good luck to George in a glass o' beer, and said she 'oped that 'er own boy would grow up like him. "Let 'im grow up a good and brave man, that's all I ask," she ses. "I don't care about 'is looks."

"He might have both," ses George, sharp-like. "Why not?"

Mrs. Mitchell said she supposed he might, and then she cuffed young Ted's ears for making a noise while 'e was eating, and then cuffed 'im agin for saying that he'd finished 'is supper five minutes ago.

George and Bob walked 'ome together, and all the way there George said wot a pretty gal Gerty was and 'ow lucky it was for Bob that he 'adn't been drownded. He went round to tea with 'im the next day to Mrs. Mitchell's, and arter tea, when Bob and Gerty said they was going out to spend the evening together, got 'imself asked too.

They took a tram-car and went to a music-hall, and Bob paid for the three of 'em. George never seemed to think of putting his 'and in his pocket, and even arter the music-hall, when they all went into a shop and 'ad stewed eels, he let Bob pay.

As I said afore, Bob Evans was chock-full of gratefulness, and it seemed only fair that he shouldn't grumble at spending a little over the man wot 'ad risked 'is life to save his; but wot with keeping George at his room, and paying for 'im every time they went out, he was spending a lot more money than 'e could afford.

"You're on'y young once, Bob," George said to him when 'e made a remark one arternoon as to the fast way his money was going, "and if it hadn't ha' been for me you'd never 'ave lived to grow old."

Wot with spending the money and always 'aving George with them when they went out, it wasn't long afore Bob and Gerty 'ad a quarrel. "I don't like a pore-spirited man," she ses. "Two's company and three's none, and, besides, why can't he pay for 'imself? He's big enough. Why should you spend your money on 'im? He never pays a farthing."

Bob explained that he couldn't say anything because 'e owed his life to George, but 'e might as well 'ave talked to a lamp-post. The more he argued the more angry Gerty got, and at last she ses, "Two's company and three's none, and if you and me can't go out without George Crofts, then me and 'im 'll go out with-out you."

She was as good as her word, too, and the next night, while Bob 'ad gone out to get some 'bacca, she went off alone with George. It was ten o'clock afore they came back agin, and Gerty's eyes were all shining and 'er cheeks as pink as roses. She shut 'er mother up like a concertina the moment she began to find fault with 'er, and at supper she sat next to George and laughed at everything 'e said.

George and Bob walked all the way 'ome arter supper without saying a word, but arter they got to their room George took a side-look at Bob, and then he ses, suddenlike, "Look 'ere! I saved your life, didn't I?"

"You did," ses Bob, "and I thank you for it."

"I saved your life," ses George agin, very solemn. "If it hadn't ha' been for me you couldn't ha' married anybody."

"That's true," ses Bob.

"Me and Gerty 'ave been having a talk," ses George, bending down to undo his boots. "We've been getting on very well together; you can't 'elp your feelings, and the long and the short of it is, the pore gal has fallen in love with me."

Bob didn't say a word.

"If you look at it this way it's fair enough," ses George. "I gave you your life and you give me your gal. We're quits now. You don't owe me anything and I don't owe you anything. That's the way Gerty puts it, and she told me to tell you so."

"If—if she don't want me I'm agreeable," ses Bob, in a choking voice. "We'll call it quits, and next time I tumble overboard I 'ope you won't be handy."

He took Gerty's photygraph out of 'is box and handed it to George. "You've got more right to it now than wot I 'ave," he ses. "I shan't go round there anymore; I shall look out for a ship to-morrow."

George Crofts said that perhaps it was the best thing he could do, and 'e asked 'im in a offhand sort o' way 'ow long the room was paid up for.

Mrs. Mitchell 'ad a few words to say about it next day, but Gerty told 'er to save 'er breath for walking upstairs. The on'y thing that George didn't like when they went out was that young Ted was with them, but Gerty said she preferred it till she knew 'im better; and she 'ad so much to say about his noble behaviour in saving life that George gave way. They went out looking at the shops, George thinking that that was the cheapest way of spending an evening, and they were as happy as possible till Gerty saw a brooch she liked so much in a window that he couldn't get 'er away.

"It is a beauty," she ses. "I don't know when I've seen a brooch I liked better. Look here! Let's all guess the price and then go in and see who's right."

They 'ad their guesses, and then they went in and asked, and as soon as Gerty found that it was only three-and-sixpence she began to feel in her pocket for 'er purse, just like your wife does when you go out with 'er, knowing all the time that it's on the mantelpiece with twopence-ha'penny and a cough lozenge in it.

"I must ha' left it at 'ome," she ses, looking at George.

"Just wot I've done," ses George, arter patting 'is pockets.

Gerty bit 'er lips and, for a minute or two, be civil to George she could not. Then she gave a little smile and took 'is arm agin, and they walked on talking and laughing till she turned round of a sudden and asked a big chap as was passing wot 'e was shoving 'er for.

"Shoving you?" ses he. "Wot do you think I want to shove you for?"

"Don't you talk to me," ses Gerty, firing up. "George, make 'im beg my pardon."

"You ought to be more careful," ses George, in a gentle sort o' way.

"Make 'im beg my pardon," ses Gerty, stamping 'er foot; "if he don't, knock 'im down."

"Yes, knock 'im down," ses the big man, taking hold o' George's cap and rumpling his 'air.

Pore George, who was never much good with his fists, hit 'im in the chest, and the next moment he was on 'is back in the middle o' the road wondering wot had 'appened to 'im. By the time 'e got up the other man was arf a mile away; and young Ted stepped up and wiped 'im down with a pocket-'andkerchief while Gerty explained to 'im 'ow she saw 'im slip on a piece o' banana peel.

"It's 'ard lines," she ses; "but never mind, you frightened 'im away, and I don't wonder at it. You do look terrible when you're angry, George; I didn't know you."

She praised 'im all the way 'ome, and if it 'adn't been for his mouth and nose George would 'ave enjoyed it more than 'e did. She told 'er mother how 'e had flown at a big man wot 'ad insulted her, and Mrs. Mitchell shook her 'ead at 'im and said his bold spirit would lead 'im into trouble afore he 'ad done.

They didn't seem to be able to make enough of 'im, and next day when he went round Gerty was so upset at the sight of 'is bruises that he thought she was going to cry. When he had 'ad his tea she gave 'im a cigar she had bought for 'im herself, and when he 'ad finished smoking it she smiled at him, and said that she was going to take 'im out for a pleasant evening to try and make up to 'im for wot he 'ad suffered for 'er.

"We're all going to stand treat to each other," she ses. "Bob always would insist on paying for everything, but I like to feel a bit independent. Give and take—that's the way I like to do things."

"There's nothing like being independent," ses George. "Bob ought to ha' known that."

"I'm sure it's the best plan," ses Gerty. "Now, get your 'at on. We're going to a theayter, and Ted shall pay the 'bus fares."

George wanted to ask about the theayter, but 'e didn't like to, and arter Gerty was dressed they went out and Ted paid the 'bus fares like a man.

"Here you are," ses Gerty, as the 'bus stopped outside the theayter. "Hurry up and get the tickets, George; ask for three upper circles."

She bustled George up to the pay place, and as soon as she 'ad picked out the seats she grabbed 'old of the tickets and told George to make haste.

"Twelve shillings it is," ses the man, as George put down arf a crown.

"Twelve?" ses George, beginning to stammer. "Twelve? Twelve? Twel—?"

"Twelve shillings," ses the man; "three upper circles you've 'ad."

George was going to fetch Gerty back and 'ave cheaper seats, but she 'ad gone inside with young Ted, and at last, arter making an awful fuss, he paid the rest o' the money and rushed in arter her, arf crazy at the idea o' spending so much money.

"Make 'aste," ses Gerty, afore he could say anything; "the band 'as just begun."

She started running upstairs, and she was so excited that, when they got their seats and George started complaining about the price, she didn't pay any attention to wot he was saying, but kept pointing out ladies' dresses to 'im in w'ispers and wondering wot they 'ad paid for them. George gave it up at last, and then he sat wondering whether he 'ad done right arter all in taking Bob's gal away from him.

Gerty enjoyed it very much, but when the curtain came down after the first act she leaned back in her chair and looked up at George and said she felt faint and thought she'd like to 'ave an ice-cream. "And you 'ave one too, dear," she ses, when young Ted 'ad got up and beckoned to the gal, "and Ted 'ud like one too, I'm sure."

She put her 'ead on George's shoulder and looked up at 'im. Then she put her 'and on his and stroked it, and George, reckoning that arter all ice-creams were on'y a ha'penny or at the most a penny each, altered 'is mind about not spending any more money and ordered three.

The way he carried on when the gal said they was three shillings was alarming. At fust 'e thought she was 'aving a joke with 'im, and it took another gal and the fireman and an old gentleman wot was sitting behind 'im to persuade 'im different. He was so upset that 'e couldn't eat his arter paying for it, and Ted and Gerty had to finish it for 'im.

"They're expensive, but they're worth the money," ses Gerty. "You are good to me, George. I could go on eating 'em all night, but you mustn't fling your money away like this always."

"I'll see to that," ses George, very bitter.

"I thought we was going to stand treat to each other? That was the idea, I understood."

"So we are," ses Gerty. "Ted stood the 'bus fares, didn't he?"

"He did," ses George, "wot there was of 'em; but wot about you?"

"Me?" ses Gerty, drawing her 'ead back and staring at 'im. "Why, 'ave you forgot that cigar already, George?"

George opened 'is mouth, but 'e couldn't speak a word. He sat looking at 'er and making a gasping noise in 'is throat, and fortunately just as 'e got 'is voice back the curtain went up agin, and everybody said, "H'sh!"

He couldn't enjoy the play at all, 'e was so upset, and he began to see more than ever 'ow wrong he 'ad been in taking Bob's gal away from 'im. He walked downstairs into the street like a man in a dream, with Gerty sticking to 'is arm and young Ted treading on 'is heels behind.

"Now, you mustn't waste any more money, George," ses Gerty, when they got outside. "We'll walk 'ome."

George 'ad got arf a mind to say something about a 'bus, but he remembered in time that very likely young Ted hadn't got any more money. Then Gerty said she knew a short cut, and she took them, walking along little, dark, narrow streets and places, until at last, just as George thought they must be pretty near 'ome, she began to dab her eyes with 'er pocket-'andkerchief and say she'd lost 'er way.

"You two go 'ome and leave me," she ses, arf crying. "I can't walk another step."

"Where are we?" ses George, looking round.

"I don't know," ses Gerty. "I couldn't tell you if you paid me. I must 'ave taken a wrong turning. Oh, hurrah! Here's a cab!"

Afore George could stop 'er she held up 'er umbrella, and a 'ansom cab, with bells on its horse, crossed the road and pulled up in front of 'em. Ted nipped in first and Gerty followed 'im.

"Tell 'im the address, dear, and make 'aste and get in," ses Gerty.

George told the cabman, and then he got in and sat on Ted's knee, partly on Gerty's umbrella, and mostly on nothing.

"You are good to me, George," ses Gerty, touching the back of 'is neck with the brim of her hat. "It ain't often I get a ride in a cab. All the time I was keeping company with Bob we never 'ad one once. I only wish I'd got the money to pay for it."

George, who was going to ask a question, stopped 'imself, and then he kept striking matches and trying to read all about cab fares on a bill in front of 'im.

"'Ow are we to know 'ow many miles it is?" he ses, at last.

"I don't know," ses Gerty; "leave it to the cabman. It's his bisness, ain't it? And if 'e don't know he must suffer for it."

There was hardly a soul in Gerty's road when they got there, but afore George 'ad settled with the cabman there was a policeman moving the crowd on and arf the winders in the road up. By the time George had paid 'im and the cabman 'ad told him wot 'e looked like, Gerty and Ted 'ad disappeared indoors, all the lights was out, and, in a state o' mind that won't bear thinking of, George walked 'ome to his lodging.

Bob was asleep when he got there, but 'e woke 'im up and told 'im about it, and then arter a time he said that he thought Bob ought to pay arf because he 'ad saved 'is life.

"Cert'nly not," ses Bob. "We're quits now; that was the arrangement. I only wish it was me spending the money on her; I shouldn't grumble."

George didn't get a wink o' sleep all night for thinking of the money he 'ad spent, and next day when he went round he 'ad almost made up 'is mind to tell Bob that if 'e liked to pay up the money he could 'ave Gerty back; but she looked so pretty, and praised 'im up so much for 'is generosity, that he began to think better of it. One thing 'e was determined on, and that was never to spend money like that agin for fifty Gertys.

There was a very sensible man there that evening that George liked very much. His name was Uncle Joe, and when Gerty was praising George to 'is face for the money he 'ad been spending, Uncle Joe, instead o' looking pleased, shook his 'ead over it.

"Young people will be young people, I know," he ses, "but still I don't approve of extravagance. Bob Evans would never 'ave spent all that money over you."

"Bob Evans ain't everybody," ses Mrs. Mitchell, standing up for Gerty.

"He was steady, anyway," ses Uncle Joe. "Besides, Gerty ought not to ha' let Mr. Crofts spend his money like that. She could ha' prevented it if she'd ha' put 'er foot down and insisted on it."

He was so solemn about it that everybody began to feel a bit upset, and Gerty borrowed Ted's pocket-'andkerchief, and then wiped 'er eyes on the cuff of her dress instead.

"Well, well," ses Uncle Joe; "I didn't mean to be 'ard, but don't do it no more. You are young people, and can't afford it."

"We must 'ave a little pleasure sometimes," ses Gerty.

"Yes, I know," ses Uncle Joe; "but there's moderation in everything. Look 'ere, it's time somebody paid for Mr. Crofts. To-morrow's Saturday, and, if you like, I'll take you all to the Crystal Palace."

Gerty jumped up off of 'er chair and kissed 'im, while Mrs. Mitchell said she knew 'is bark was worse than 'is bite, and asked 'im who was wasting his money now?

"You meet me at London Bridge Station at two o'clock," ses Uncle Joe, getting up to go. "It ain't extravagance for a man as can afford it."

He shook 'ands with George Crofts and went, and, arter George 'ad stayed long enough to hear a lot o' things about Uncle Joe which made 'im think they'd get on very well together, he went off too.

They all turned up very early the next arternoon, and Gerty was dressed so nice that George couldn't take his eyes off of her. Besides her there was Mrs. Mitchell and Ted and a friend of 'is named Charlie Smith.

They waited some time, but Uncle Joe didn't turn up, and they all got looking at the clock and talking about it, and 'oping he wouldn't make 'em miss the train.

"Here he comes!" ses Ted, at last.

Uncle Joe came rushing in, puffing and blowing as though he'd bust. "Take 'em on by this train, will you?" he ses, catching 'old o' George by the arm. "I've just been stopped by a bit o' business I must do, and I'll come on by the next, or as soon arter as I can."

He rushed off again, puffing and blowing his 'ardest, in such a hurry that he forgot to give George the money for the tickets. However, George borrowed a pencil of Mrs. Mitchell in the train, and put down on paper 'ow much they cost, and Mrs. Mitchell said if George didn't like to remind 'im she would.

They left young Ted and Charlie to stay near the station when they got to the Palace, Uncle Joe 'aving forgotten to say where he'd meet 'em, but train arter train came in without 'im, and at last the two boys gave it up.

"We're sure to run across 'im sooner or later," ses Gerty. "Let's 'ave something to eat; I'm so hungry."

George said something about buns and milk, but Gerty took 'im up sharp. "Buns and milk?" she ses. "Why, uncle would never forgive us if we spoilt his treat like that."

She walked into a refreshment place and they 'ad cold meat and bread and pickles and beer and tarts and cheese, till even young Ted said he'd 'ad enough, but still they couldn't see any signs of Uncle Joe. They went on to the roundabouts to look for 'im, and then into all sorts o' shows at sixpence a head, but still there was no signs of 'im, and George had 'ad to start on a fresh bit o' paper to put down wot he'd spent.

"I suppose he must ha' been detained on important business," ses Gerty, at last.

"Unless it's one of 'is jokes," ses Mrs. Mitchell, shaking her 'ead. "You know wot your uncle is, Gerty."

"There now, I never thought o' that," ses Gerty, with a start; "p'r'aps it is."

"Joke?" ses George, choking and staring from one to the other.

"I was wondering where he'd get the money from," ses Mrs. Mitchell to Gerty. "I see it all now; I never see such a man for a bit o' fun in all my born days. And the solemn way he went on last night, too. Why, he must ha' been laughing in 'is sleeve all the time. It's as good as a play."

"Look here!" ses George, 'ardly able to speak; "do you mean to tell me he never meant to come?"

"I'm afraid not," ses Mrs. Mitchell, "knowing wot he is. But don't you worry; I'll give him a bit o' my mind when I see 'im."

George Crofts felt as though he'd burst, and then 'e got his breath, and the things 'e said about Uncle Joe was so awful that Mrs. Mitchell told the boys to go away.

"How dare you talk of my uncle like that?" ses Gerty, firing up.

"You forget yourself, George," ses Mrs. Mitchell. "You'll like 'im when you get to know 'im better."

"Don't you call me George," ses George Crofts, turning on 'er. "I've been done, that's wot I've been. I 'ad fourteen pounds when I was paid off, and it's melting like butter."

"Well, we've enjoyed ourselves," ses Gerty, "and that's what money was given us for. I'm sure those two boys 'ave had a splendid time, thanks to you. Don't go and spoil all by a little bit o' temper."

"Temper!" ses George, turning on her. "I've done with you, I wouldn't marry you if you was the on'y gal in the world. I wouldn't marry you if you paid me."

"Oh, indeed!" ses Gerty; "but if you think you can get out of it like that you're mistaken. I've lost my young man through you, and I'm not going to lose you too. I'll send my two big cousins round to see you to-morrow."

"They won't put up with no nonsense, I can tell you," ses Mrs. Mitchell.

She called the boys to her, and then she and Gerty, arter holding their 'eads very high and staring at George, went off and left 'im alone. He went straight off 'ome, counting 'is money all the way and trying to make it more, and, arter telling Bob 'ow he'd been treated, and trying hard to get 'im to go shares in his losses, packed up his things and cleared out, all boiling over with temper.

Bob was so dazed he couldn't make head or tail out of it, but 'e went round to see Gerty the first thing next morning, and she explained things to him.

"I don't know when I've enjoyed myself so much," she ses, wiping her eyes, "but I've had enough gadding about for once, and if you come round this evening we'll have a nice quiet time together looking at the furniture shops."

BREAKING A SPELL

"Witchcraft?" said the old man, thoughtfully, as he scratched his scanty whiskers. No, I ain't heard o' none in these parts for a long time. There used to be a little of it about when I was a boy, and there was some talk of it arter I'd growed up, but Claybury folk never took much count of it. The last bit of it I remember was about forty years ago, and that wasn't so much witchcraft as foolishness.

There was a man in this place then—Joe Barlcomb by name—who was a firm believer in it, and 'e used to do all sorts of things to save hisself from it. He was a new-comer in Claybury, and there was such a lot of it about in the parts he came from that the people thought o' nothing else hardly.

He was a man as got 'imself very much liked at fust, especially by the old ladies, owing to his being so perlite to them, that they used to 'old 'im up for an example to the other men, and say wot nice, pretty ways he 'ad. Joe Barlcomb was everything at fust, but when they got to 'ear that his perliteness was because 'e thought 'arf of 'em was witches, and didn't know which 'arf, they altered their minds.

In a month or two he was the laughing-stock of the place; but wot was worse to 'im than that was that he'd made enemies of all the old ladies. Some of 'em was free-spoken women, and 'e couldn't sleep for thinking of the 'arm they might do 'im.

He was terrible uneasy about it at fust, but, as nothing 'appened and he seemed to go on very prosperous-like, 'e began to forget 'is fears, when all of a sudden 'e went 'ome one day and found 'is wife in bed with a broken leg.

She was standing on a broken chair to reach something down from the dresser when it 'appened, and it was pointed out to Joe Barlcomb that it was a thing anybody might ha' done without being bewitched; but he said 'e knew better, and that they'd kept that broken chair for standing on for years and years to save the others, and nothing 'ad ever 'appened afore.

In less than a week arter that three of his young 'uns was down with the measles, and, 'is wife being laid up, he sent for 'er mother to come and nurse 'em. It's as true as I sit 'ere, but that pore old lady 'adn't been in the house two hours afore she went to bed with the yellow jaundice.

Joe Barlcomb went out of 'is mind a'most. He'd never liked 'is wife's mother, and he wouldn't 'ave had 'er in the house on'y 'e wanted her to nurse 'is wife and children, and when she came and laid up and wanted waiting on 'e couldn't dislike her enough.

He was quite certain all along that somebody was putting a spell on 'im, and when 'e went out a morning or two arterward and found 'is best pig lying dead in a corner of the sty he gave up and, going into the 'ouse, told 'em all that they'd 'ave to die 'cause he couldn't do anything more for 'em. His wife's mother and 'is wife and the children all started crying together, and Joe Barlcomb, when 'e thought of 'is pig, he sat down and cried too.

He sat up late that night thinking it over, and, arter looking at it all ways, he made up 'is mind to go and see Mrs. Prince, an old lady that lived all alone by 'erself in a cottage near Smith's farm. He'd set 'er down for wot he called a white witch, which is the best kind and on'y do useful things, such as charming warts away or telling gals about their future 'usbands; and the next arternoon, arter telling 'is wife's mother that fresh air and travelling was the best cure for the yellow jaundice, he set off to see 'er.

Mrs. Prince was sitting at 'er front door nursing 'er three cats when 'e got there. She was an ugly, little old woman with piercing black eyes and a hook nose, and she 'ad a quiet, artful sort of a way with 'er that made 'er very much disliked. One thing was she was always making fun of people, and for another she seemed to be able to tell their thoughts, and that don't get anybody liked much, especially when they don't keep it to theirselves. She'd been a lady's maid all 'er young days, and it was very 'ard to be taken for a witch just because she was old.

"Fine day, ma'am," ses Joe Barlcomb.

"Very fine," ses Mrs. Prince.

"Being as I was passing, I just thought I'd look in," ses Joe Barlcomb, eyeing the cats.

"Take a chair," ses Mrs. Prince, getting up and dusting one down with 'er apron.

Joe sat down. "I'm in a bit o' trouble, ma'am," he ses, "and I thought p'r'aps as you could help me out of it. My pore pig's been bewitched, and it's dead."

"Bewitched?" ses Mrs. Prince, who'd 'eard of 'is ideas. "Rubbish. Don't talk to me."

"It ain't rubbish, ma'am," ses Joe Barlcomb; "three o' my children is down with the measles, my wife's broke 'er leg, 'er mother is laid up in my little place with the yellow jaundice, and the pig's dead."

"Wot, another one?" ses Mrs. Prince.

"No; the same one," ses Joe.

"Well, 'ow am I to help you?" ses Mrs. Prince. "Do you want me to come and nurse 'em?"

"No, no," ses Joe, starting and turning pale; "unless you'd like to come and nurse my wife's mother," he ses, arter thinking a bit. "I was hoping that you'd know who'd been overlooking me and that you'd make 'em take the spell off."

Mrs. Prince got up from 'er chair and looked round for the broom she'd been sweeping with, but, not finding it, she set down agin and stared in a curious sort o' way at Joe Barlcomb.

"Oh, I see," she ses, nodding. "Fancy you guessing I was a witch."

"You can't deceive me," ses Joe; "I've 'ad too much experience; I knew it the fust time I saw you by the mole on your nose."

Mrs. Prince got up and went into her back-place, trying her 'ardest to remember wot she'd done with that broom. She couldn't find it anywhere, and at last she came back and sat staring at Joe for so long that 'e was 'arf frightened out of his life. And by-and-by she gave a 'orrible smile and sat rubbing the side of 'er nose with 'er finger.

"If I help you," she ses at last, "will you promise to keep it a dead secret and do exactly as I tell you? If you don't, dead pigs'll be nothing to the misfortunes that you will 'ave."

"I will," ses Joe Barlcomb, very pale.

"The spell," ses Mrs. Prince, holding up her 'ands and shutting 'er eyes, "was put upon you by a man. It is one out of six men as is jealous of you because you're so clever, but which one it is I can't tell without your assistance. Have you got any money?"

"A little," ses Joe, anxious-like—"a very little. Wot with the yellow jaundice and other things, I—"

"Fust thing to do," ses Mrs. Prince, still with her eyes shut, "you go up to the Cauliflower to-night; the six men'll all be there, and you must buy six ha'pennies off of them; one each."

"Buy six ha'pennies?" ses Joe, staring at her.

"Don't repeat wot I say," ses Mrs. Prince; "it's unlucky. You buy six ha'pennies for a shilling each, without saying wot it's for. You'll be able to buy 'em all right if you're civil."

"It seems to me it don't need much civility for that," ses Joe, pulling a long face.

"When you've got the ha'pennies," ses Mrs. Prince, "bring 'em to me and I'll tell you wot to do with 'em. Don't lose no time, because I can see that something worse is going to 'appen if it ain't prevented."

"Is it anything to do with my wife's mother getting worse?" ses Joe Barlcomb, who was a careful man and didn't want to waste six shillings.

"No, something to you," ses Mrs. Prince.

Joe Barlcomb went cold all over, and then he put down a couple of eggs he'd brought round for 'er and went off 'ome agin, and Mrs. Prince stood in the doorway with a cat on each shoulder and watched 'im till 'e was out of sight.

That night Joe Barlcomb came up to this 'ere Cauliflower public-house, same as he'd been told, and by-and-by, arter he 'ad 'ad a pint, he looked round, and taking a shilling out of 'is pocket put it on the table, and he ses, "Who'll give me a ha'penny for that?" he ses.

None of 'em seemed to be in a hurry. Bill Jones took it up and bit it, and rang it on the table and squinted at it, and then he bit it again, and turned round and asked Joe Barlcomb wot was wrong with it.

"Wrong?" ses Joe; "nothing."

Bill Jones put it down agin. "You're wide awake, Joe," he ses, "but so am I."

"Won't nobody give me a ha'penny for it?" ses Joe, looking round.

Then Peter Lamb came up, and he looked at it and rang it, and at last he gave Joe a ha'penny for it and took it round, and everybody 'ad a look at it.

"It stands to reason it's a bad 'un," ses Bill Jones, "but it's so well done I wish as I'd bought it."

"H-s-h!" ses Peter Lamb; "don't let the landlord 'ear you."

The landlord 'ad just that moment come in, and Peter walked up and ordered a pint, and took his ten-pence change as bold as brass. Arter that Joe Barbcomb bought five more ha'pennies afore you could wink a'most, and every man wot sold one went up to the bar and 'ad a pint and got tenpence change, and drank Joe Barlcomb's health.

"There seems to be a lot o' money knocking about to-night," ses the landlord, as Sam Martin, the last of 'em, was drinking 'is pint.

Sam Martin choked and put 'is pot down on the counter with a bang, and him and the other five was out o' that door and sailing up the road with their tenpences afore the landlord could get his breath. He stood to the bar scratching his 'ead and staring, but he couldn't understand it a bit till a man wot was too late to sell his ha'penny up and told 'im all about it. The fuss 'e made was terrible. The shillings was in a little heap on a shelf at the back o' the bar, and he did all sorts o' things to 'em to prove that they was bad, and threatened Joe Barlcomb with the police. At last, however, 'e saw wot a fool he was making of himself, and arter nearly breaking his teeth 'e dropped them into a drawer and stirred 'em up with the others.

Joe Barlcomb went round the next night to see Mrs. Prince, and she asked 'im a lot o' questions about the men as 'ad sold 'im the ha'pennies.

"The fust part 'as been done very well," she ses, nodding her 'ead at 'im; "if you do the second part as well, you'll soon know who your enemy is."

"Nothing'll bring the pig back," ses Joe.

"There's worse misfortunes than that, as I've told you," ses Mrs. Prince, sharply. "Now, listen to wot I'm going to say to you. When the clock strikes twelve to-night—"

"Our clock don't strike," ses Joe.

"Then you must borrow one that does," ses Mrs. Prince, "and when it strikes twelve you must go round to each o' them six men and sell them a ha'penny for a shilling."

Joe Barlcomb looked at 'er. "'Ow?" he ses, short-like.

"Same way as you sold 'em a shilling for a ha'-penny," ses Mrs. Prince; "it don't matter whether they buy the ha'pennies or not. All you've got to do is to go and ask 'em, and the man as makes the most fuss is the man that 'as put the trouble on you."

"It seems a roundabout way o' going to work," ses Joe.

"*Wot!*" screams Mrs. Prince, jumping up and waving her arms about. "*Wot!* Go your own way; I'll have nothing more to do with you. And don't blame me for anything that happens. It's a very bad thing to come to a witch for advice and then not to do as she tells you. You ought to know that."

"I'll do it, ma'am," ses Joe Barlcomb, trembling.

"You'd better," ses Mrs. Prince; "and mind—not a word to anybody."

Joe promised her agin, and 'e went off and borrered a clock from Albert Price, and at twelve o'clock that night he jumped up out of bed and began to dress 'imself and pretend not to 'ear his wife when she asked 'im where he was going.

It was a dark, nasty sort o' night, blowing and raining, and, o' course, everybody 'ad gone to bed long since. The fust cottage Joe came to was Bill Jones's, and, knowing Bill's temper, he stood for some time afore he could make up 'is mind to knock; but at last he up with 'is stick and banged away at the door.

A minute arterward he 'eard the bedroom winder pushed open, and then Bill Jones popped his 'cad out and called to know wot was the matter and who it was.

"It's me—Joe Barlcomb," ses Joe, "and I want to speak to you very partikler."

"Well, speak away," ses Bill. "You go into the back room," he ses, turning to his wife.

"Whaffor?" ses Mrs. Jones.

"'Cos I don't know wot Joe is going to say," ses Bill. "You go in now, afore I make you."

His wife went off grumbling, and then Bill told Joe Barlcomb to hurry up wot he'd got to say as 'e 'adn't got much on and the weather wasn't as warm as it might be.

"I sold you a shilling for a ha'penny last night, Bill," ses Joe.

"Do you want to sell any more?" ses Bill Jones, putting his 'and down to where 'is trouser pocket ought to be.

"Not exactly that," ses Joe Barlcomb. "This time I want you to sell me a shilling for a ha'penny."

Bill leaned out of the winder and stared down at Joe Barlcomb, and then he ses, in a choking voice, "Is that wot you've come disturbing my sleep for at this time o' night?" he ses.

"I must 'ave it, Bill," ses Joe.

"Well, if you'll wait a moment," ses Bill, trying to speak perlitely, "I'll come down and give it to you."

Joe didn't like 'is tone of voice, but he waited, and all of a sudden Bill Jones came out o' that door like a gun going off and threw 'imself on Joe Barlcomb. Both of 'em was strong men, and by the time they'd finished they was so tired they could 'ardly stand. Then Bill Jones went back to bed, and Joe Barlcomb, arter sitting down on the doorstep to rest 'imself, went off and knocked up Peter Lamb.

Peter Lamb was a little man and no good as a fighter, but the things he said to Joe Barlcomb as he leaned out o' the winder and shook 'is fist at him was 'arder to bear than blows. He screamed away at the top of 'is voice for ten minutes, and then 'e pulled the winder to with a bang and went back to bed.

Joe Barlcomb was very tired, but he walked on to Jasper Potts's 'ouse, trying 'ard as he walked to decide which o' the fust two 'ad made the most fuss. Arter he 'ad left Jasper Potts 'e got more puzzled than ever, Jasper being just as bad as the other two, and Joe leaving 'im at last in the middle of loading 'is gun.

By the time he'd made 'is last call—at Sam Martin's—it was past three o'clock, and he could no more tell Mrs. Prince which 'ad made the most fuss than 'e could fly. There didn't seem to be a pin to choose between 'em, and, 'arf worried out of 'is life, he went straight on to Mrs. Prince and knocked 'er up to tell 'er. She thought the 'ouse was afire at fust, and came screaming out o' the front door in 'er bedgown, and when she found out who it was she was worse to deal with than the men 'ad been.

She 'ad quieted down by the time Joe went round to see 'er the next evening, and asked 'im to describe exactly wot the six men 'ad done and said. She sat listening quite quiet at fust, but arter a time she scared Joe by making a odd, croupy sort o' noise in 'er throat, and at last she got up and walked into the back-place. She was there a long time making funny noises, and at last Joe walked toward the door on tip-toe and peeped through the crack and saw 'er in a sort o' fit, sitting in a chair with 'er arms folded acrost her bodice and rocking 'erself up and down and moaning. Joe stood as if 'e'd been frozen a'most, and then 'e crept back to 'is seat and waited, and when she came into the room agin she said as the trouble 'ad all been caused by Bill Jones. She sat still for nearly 'arf an hour, thinking 'ard, and then she turned to Joe and ses:

"Can you read?" she ses.

"No," ses Joe, wondering wot was coming next.

"That's all right, then," she ses, "because if you could I couldn't do wot I'm going to do."

"That shows the 'arm of eddication," ses Joe. "I never did believe in it."

Mrs. Prince nodded, and then she went and got a bottle with something in it which looked to Joe like gin, and arter getting out 'er pen and ink and printing some words on a piece o' paper she stuck it on the bottle, and sat looking at Joe and thinking.

"Take this up to the Cauliflower," she ses, "make friends with Bill Jones, and give him as much beer as he'll drink, and give 'im a little o' this gin in each mug. If he drinks it the spell will be broken, and you'll be luckier than you 'ave ever been in your life afore. When 'e's drunk some, and not before, leave the bottle standing on the table."

Joe Barlcomb thanked 'er, and with the bottle in 'is pocket went off to the Cauliflower, whistling. Bill Jones was there, and Peter Lamb, and two or three more of 'em, and at fust they said some pretty 'ard things to him about being woke up in the night.

"Don't bear malice, Bill," ses Joe Barlcomb; "'ave a pint with me."

He ordered two pints, and then sat down along-side o' Bill, and in five minutes they was like brothers.

"'Ave a drop o' gin in it, Bill," he ses, taking the bottle out of 'is pocket.

Bill thanked 'im and had a drop, and then, thoughtful-like, he wanted Joe to 'ave some in his too, but Joe said no, he'd got a touch o' toothache, and it was bad for it.

"I don't mind 'aving a drop in my beer, Joe," ses Peter Lamb.

"Not to-night, mate," ses Joe; "it's all for Bill. I bought it on purpose for 'im."

Bill shook 'ands with him, and when Joe called for another pint and put some more gin in it he said that 'e was the noblest-'arted man that ever lived.

"You wasn't saying so 'arf an hour ago," ses Peter Lamb.

"'Cos I didn't know 'im so well then," ses Bill Jones.

"You soon change your mind, don't you?" ses Peter.

Bill didn't answer 'im. He was leaning back on the bench and staring at the bottle as if 'e couldn't believe his eyesight. His face was all white and shining, and 'is hair as wet as if it 'ad just been dipped in a bucket o' water.

"See a ghost, Bill?" ses Peter, looking at 'im.

Bill made a 'orrible noise in his throat, and kept on staring at the bottle till they thought 'e'd gone crazy. Then Jasper Potts bent his 'ead down and began to read out loud wot was on the bottle. "P-o-i—POISON FOR BILL JONES," he ses, in a voice as if 'e couldn't believe it.

You might 'ave heard a pin drop. Everybody turned and looked at Bill Jones, as he sat there trembling all over. Then those that could read took up the bottle and read it out loud all over agin.

"Pore Bill," ses Peter Lamb. "I 'ad a feeling come over me that something was wrong."

"You're a murderer," ses Sam Martin, catching 'old of Joe Barlcomb. "You'll be 'ung for this. Look at pore Bill, cut off in 'is prime."

"Run for the doctor," ses someone.

Two of 'em ran off as 'ard as they could go, and then the landlord came round the bar and asked Bill to go and die outside, because 'e didn't want to be brought into it. Jasper Potts told 'im to clear off, and then he bent down and asked Bill where the pain was.

"I don't think he'll 'ave much pain," ses Peter Lamb, who always pretended to know a lot more than other people. "It'll soon be over, Bill."

"We've all got to go some day," ses Sam Martin. "Better to die young than live to be a trouble to yourself," ses Bob Harris.

To 'ear them talk everybody seemed to think that Bill Jones was in luck; everybody but Bill Jones 'imself, that is.

"I ain't fit to die," he ses, shivering. "You don't know 'ow bad I've been."

"Wot 'ave you done, Bill?" ses Peter Lamb, in a soft voice. "If it'll ease your feelings afore you go to make a clean breast of it, we're all friends here."

Bill groaned.

"And it's too late for you to be punished for anything," ses Peter, arter a moment.

Bill Jones groaned agin, and then, shaking 'is 'ead, began to w'isper 'is wrong-doings. When the doctor came in 'arf an hour arterward all the men was as quiet as mice, and pore Bill was still w'ispering as 'ard as he could w'isper.

The doctor pushed 'em out of the way in a moment, and then 'e bent over Bill and felt 'is pulse and looked at 'is tongue. Then he listened to his 'art, and in a puzzled way smelt at the bottle, which Jasper Potts was a-minding of, and wetted 'is finger and tasted it.

"Somebody's been making a fool of you and me too," he ses, in a angry voice. "It's only gin, and very good gin at that. Get up and go home."

It all came out next morning, and Joe Barlcomb was the laughing-stock of the place. Most people said that Mrs. Prince 'ad done quite right, and they 'oped that it ud be a lesson to him, but nobody ever talked much of witchcraft in Claybury agin. One thing was that Bill Jones wouldn't 'ave the word used in 'is hearing.

BREVET RANK

The crew of the Elisabeth Hopkins sat on deck in the gloaming, gazing idly at the dusky shapes of the barges as they dropped silently down on the tide, or violently discussing the identity of various steamers as they came swiftly past Even with these amusements the time hung heavily, and they thought longingly of certain cosy bars by the riverside to which they were wont to betake themselves in their spare time.

To-night, in deference to the wishes of the skipper, wishes which approximated closely to those of Royalty in their effects, they remained on board. A new acquaintance of his, a brother captain, who dabbled in mesmerism, was coming to give them a taste of his quality, and the skipper, sitting on the side of the schooner in the faint light which streamed from the galley, was condescendingly explaining to them the marvels of hypnotism.

"I never 'eard the likes of it," said one, with a deep breath, as the skipper concluded a marvellous example.

"There's a lot you ain't 'eard of, Bill," said another, whose temper was suffering from lack of beer. "But 'ave you seen all this, sir?"

"Everything," said the skipper, impressively. "He wanted to mesmerise me, an' I said, 'All right,' I ses, 'do it an' welcome—if you can, but I expect my head's a bit too strong for you.'"

"And it was, sir, I'll bet," said the man who had been so candid with Bill.

"He tried everything," said the skipper, "then he give it up; but he's coming aboard to-night, so any of you that likes can come down the cabin and be mesmerised free."

"Why can't he do it on deck?" said the mate, rising from the hatches and stretching his gigantic form.

"'Cos he must have artificial light, George," said the skipper. "He lets me a little bit into the secret, you know, an' he told me he likes to have the men a bit dazed-like first."

Voices sounded from the wharf, and the night-watchman appeared piloting Captain Zingall to the schooner. The crew noticed that he came aboard quite like any other man, descending the ladder with even more care than usual. He was a small man, of much dignity, with light grey eyes which had been so strained by the exercise of his favourite hobby that they appeared to be starting from his head. He chatted agreeably about freights for some time, and then, at his brother skipper's urgent entreaty, consented to go below and give them a taste of his awful powers.

At first he was not very successful. The men stared at the discs he put into their hands until their eyes ached, but for some time without effect. Bill was the first to yield, and to the astonishment of his friends passed into a soft magnetic slumber, from which he emerged to perform the usual idiotic tricks peculiar to mesmerised subjects.

"It's wonderful what power you 'ave over em," said Captain Bradd, respectfully.

Captain Zingall smiled affably. "At the present moment," he said, "that man is my unthinkin' slave, an' whatever I wish him to do he does. Would any of you like him to do anything?"

"Well, sir," said one of the men, "'e owes me 'arf a crown, an' I think it would be a 'ighly interestin' experiment if you could get 'im to pay me. If anything 'ud make me believe in mesmerism, that would."

"An' he owes me eighteenpence, sir," said another seaman, eagerly.

"One at a time," said the first speaker, sharply.

"An' 'e's owed me five shillin's since I don't know when," said the cook, with dishonest truthfulness.

Captain Zingall turned to his subject. "You owe that man half a crown," he said, pointing, "that one eighteenpence, and that one five shillings. Pay them."

In the most matter-of-fact way in the world Bill groped in his pockets, and, producing some greasy coins, payed the sums mentioned, to the intense delight of everybody.

"Well, I'm blest," said the mate, staring. "I thought mesmerism was all rubbish. Now bring him to again."

"But don't tell 'im wot 'e's been doin'," said the cook.

Zingall with a few passes brought his subject round, and with a subdued air he took his place with the others.

"What'd it feel like, Bill?" asked Joe. "Can you remember what you did?"

Bill shook his head.

"Don't try to," said the cook, feelingly.

"I should like to put you under the influence," said Zingall, eyeing the mate.

"You couldn't," said that gentleman, promptly.

"Let me try," said Zingall, persuasively.

"Do," said the skipper, "to oblige me, George."

"Well, I don't mind much," said the mate, hesitating; "but no making me give those chaps money, you know."

"No, no," said Zingall.

"Wot does 'e mean? Give the chaps money?" said Bill, turning with a startled air to the cook.

"I dunno," said the cook airily. "Just watch 'im, Bill," he added, anxiously.

But Bill had something better to do, and feeling in his pockets hurriedly strove to balance his cash account. It was impossible to do anything else while he was doing it, and the situation became so strained and his language so weird that the skipper was compelled in the interest of law and morality to order him from the cabin.

"Look at me," said Zingall to the mate after quiet had been restored.

The mate complied, and everybody gazed spellbound at the tussle for supremacy between brute force and occult science. Slowly, very slowly, science triumphed, being interrupted several times by the blood-curdling threats of Bill, as they floated down the companion-way. Then the mate suddenly lurched forward, and would have fallen but that strong hands caught him and restored him to his seat.

"I'm going to show you something now, if I can," said Zingall, wiping his brow; "but I don't know how it'll come off, because I'm only a beginner at this sort of thing, and I've never tried this before. If you don't mind, cap'n, I'm going to tell him he is Cap'n Bradd, and that you are the mate."

"Go ahead," said the delighted Bradd.

Captain Zingall went ahead full speed. With a few rapid passes he roused the mate from his torpor and fixed him with his glittering eye.

"You are Cap'n Bradd, master o' this ship," he said slowly.

"Ay, ay," said the mate, earnestly.

"And that's your mate, George, said Zingall, pointing to the deeply interested Bradd.

"Ay, ay," said the mate again, with a sigh.

"Take command, then," said Zingall, leaving him with a satisfied air and seating himself on the locker.

The mate sat up and looked about him with an air of quiet authority.

"George," he said, turning suddenly to the skipper with a very passable imitation of his voice.

"Sir," said the skipper, with a playful glance at Zingall.

"A friend o' mine named Cap'n Zingall is coming aboard to-night," said the mate, slowly. "Get a little whisky for him out o' my state-room."

"Ay, ay, sir," said the amused Bradd.

"Just a little in the bottom of the bottle 'll do," continued the mate; "don't put more in, for he drinks like a fish."

"I never said such a thing, cap'n," said Bradd, in an agitated whisper. "I never thought o' such a thing."

"No, I know you wouldn't," said Zingall, who was staring hard at a nearly empty whisky bottle on the table.

"And don't leave your baccy pouch lying about, George," continued the mate, in a thrilling whisper.

The skipper gave a faint, mirthless little laugh, and looked at him uneasily.

"If ever there was a sponger for baccy, George, it's him," said the mate, in a confidential whisper.

Captain Zingall, who was at that very moment filling his pipe from the pouch which the skipper had himself pushed towards him, laid it carefully on the table again, and gazing steadily at his friend, took out the tobacco already in his pipe and replaced it. In the silence which ensued the mate took up the whisky bottle, and pouring the contents into a tumbler, added a little water, and drank it with relish.

He leaned back on the locker and smacked his lips. There was a faint laugh from one of the crew, and looking up smartly he seemed to be aware for the first time of their presence. "What are you doin' down here?" he roared. "What do you want?"

"Nothin', sir," said the cook. "Only we thought—"

"Get out at once," vociferated the mate, rising.

"Stay where you are," said the skipper, sharply.

"George!" said the mate, in the squeaky voice in which he chose to personate the skipper.

"Bring him round, Zingall," said the skipper, irritably. "I've had enough o' this. I'll let 'im know who's who."

With a confident smile Zingall got up quietly from the locker, and fixed his terrible gaze on the mate. The mate fell back and gazed at him open-mouthed.

"Who the devil are you staring at?" he demanded, rudely.

Still holding him with his gaze, Zingall clapped his hands together, and stepping up to him blew strongly in his face. The mate, with a perfect scream of rage, picked him up by the middle, and dumping him heavily on the floor, held him there and worried him.

"Help!" cried Zingall, in a smothered voice; "take him off!"

"Why don't you bring him round?" yelled the skipper, excitably. "What's the good of playing with him?"

Zingall's reply, which was quite irrelevant, consisted almost entirely of adjectives and improper nouns.

"Blow in 'is face agin, sir," said the cook, bending down kindly.

"Take him off!" yelled Zingall; "he's killing me!"

The skipper flew to the assistance of his friend, but the mate, who was of gigantic strength and stature, simply backed, and crushed him against a bulkhead. Then, as if satisfied, he released the crestfallen Zingall, and stood looking at him.

"Why—don't—you—bring—him—round?" panted the skipper.

"He's out of my control," said Zingall, rising nimbly to his feet. "I've heard of such cases before. I'm only new at the work, you know, but I dare say, in a couple of years' time—"

The skipper howled at him, and the mate, suddenly alive again to the obnoxious presence of the crew, drove them up the companion ladder, and pursued them to the forecastle.

"This is a pretty kettle o' fish," said Bradd, indignantly. "Why don't you bring him round?"

"Because I can't," said Zingall, shortly. "It'll have to wear off."

"Wear off!" repeated the skipper.

"He's under a delusion now," said Zingall, "an' o' course I can't say how long it'll last, but whatever you do don't cross him in any way."

"Oh, don't cross him," repeated Bradd, with sarcastic inflection, "and you call yourself a mesmerist."

Zingall drew himself up with a little pride. "Well, see what I've done," he said. "The fact is, I was charged full with electricity when I came aboard, and he's got it all now. It's left me weak, and until my will wears off him he's captain o' this ship."

"And what about me?" said Bradd.

"You're the mate," said Zingall, "and mind, for your own sake, you act up to it. If you don't cross him I haven't any doubt it'll be all right, but if you do he'll very likely murder you in a fit of frenzy, and— he wouldn't be responsible. Goodnight."

"You're not going?" said Bradd, clutching him by the sleeve.

"I am," said the other. "He seems to have took a violent dislike to me, and if I stay here it'll only make him worse."

He ran lightly up on deck, and avoiding an ugly rush on the part of the mate, who had been listening, sprang on to the ladder and hastily clambered ashore.

The skipper, worn and scared, looked up as the bogus skipper came below.

"I'm going to bed, George," said the mate, staring at him. "I feel a bit heavy. Give me a call just afore high water."

"Where are you goin' to sleep?" demanded the skipper.

"Goin' to sleep?" said the mate, "why, in my state-room, to be sure."

He took the empty bottle from the table, and opening the door of the state-room, closed it in the face of its frenzied owner, and turned the key in the lock. Then he leaned over the berth, and, cramming the pillow against his mouth, gave way to his feelings until he was nearly suffocated.

Any idea that the skipper might have had of the healing effects of sleep were rudely dispelled when the mate came on deck next morning, and found that they had taken the schooner out without arousing him. His delusion seemed to be stronger than ever, and pushing the skipper from the wheel he took it himself, and read him a short and sharp lecture on the virtues of obedience.

"I know you're a good sort, George Smith," he said, leniently, "nobody could wish for a better, but while I'm master of this here ship it don't become you to take things upon yourself in the way you do."

"But you don't understand," said the skipper, trying to conquer his temper. "Now look me in the eye, George."

"Who are you calling George?" said the mate sharply.

"Well, look me in the eye, then," said the skipper, waiving the point.

"I'll look at you in a way you won't like in a minute," said the mate, ferociously.

"I want to explain the position of affairs to you," said the skipper. "Do you remember Cap'n Zingall what was aboard last night?"

"Little dirty-looking man what kept staring at me?" demanded the mate.

"Well, I don't know about 'is being dirty," said the skipper, "but that's the man. Do you know what he did to you, Geo—"

"Eh!" said the mate, sharply.

"He mesmerised you," said the skipper, hastily. "Now keep quite calm. You say you're Benjamin Bradd, master o' this vessel, don't you?"

"I do," said the mate. "Let me hear anybody say as I ain't."

"Yesterday," said the skipper, plucking up courage and speaking very slowly and impressively, "you were George Smith, the mate, but my friend, Captain Zingall, mesmerised you and made you think you were me."

"I see what it is," said the mate severely. "You've been drinking; you've been up to my whisky."

"Call the crew up and ask 'em then," said Bradd, desperately.

"Call 'em up yourself, you lunatic," said the mate, loudly enough for the men to hear. "If anybody dares to play the fool with me I won't leave a whole bone in his body, that's all."

In obedience to the summons of Captain Bradd the crew came up, and being requested by him to tell the mate that he was the mate, and that he was at present labouring under a delusion, stood silently nudging each other and eyeing him uneasily.

"Well," said the latter at length, "why don't you speak and tell George he's gone off his 'ead a bit?"

"It ain't nothing to do with us, sir," said Bill, very respectfully.

"But, damn it all, man," said the mate, taking a mighty grip of his collar, "you know I'm the cap'n, don't you?"

"O' course I do, sir," said Bill.

"There you are, George," said the mate, releasing him, and turning to the frantic Bradd; "you hear that? Now, look here, you listen to me. Either you've been drinking, or else your 'ead's gone a little bit off. You go down and turn in, and if you don't give me any more of your nonsense I'll overlook it for this once."

He ordered the crew forward again, and being desirous of leaving some permanent mark of his command on the ship, had the galley fresh painted in red and blue, and a lot of old stores, which he had vainly condemned when mate, thrown overboard. The skipper stood by helplessly while it was done, and then went below of his own accord and turned in, as being the only way to retain his sanity, or, at any rate, the clearness of head which he felt to be indispensable at this juncture.

Time, instead of restoring the mate to his senses, only appeared to confirm him in his folly, and the skipper, after another attempt to convince him, let things drift, resolving to have him put under restraint as soon as they got to port.

They reached Tidescroft in the early afternoon, but before they entered the harbour the mate, as though he had had some subtle intuition that this would be his last command, called the crew to him and read them a touching little homily upon their behaviour when they should land. He warned them of public-houses and other dangers, and reminded them affectingly of their duties as husbands and fathers. "Always go home to your wife and children, my lads," he continued with some emotion, "as I go home to mine."

"Why, he ain't got none," whispered Bill, staring.

"Don't be a fool, Bill," said the cook, "he means the cap'n's. Don't you see he's the cap'n now."

It was as clear as noonday, and the agitation of the skipper—a perfect Othello in his way—was awful. He paced the deck incessantly, casting fretful glances ashore, and, as the schooner touched the side of the quay, sprang on to the bulwarks and jumped ashore. The mate watched him with an ill-concealed grin, and then, having made the vessel snug, went below to strengthen himself with a drop of the skipper's whisky for the crowning scene of his play. He came on deck again, and, taking no heed of the whispers of the crew, went ashore.

Meantime, Captain Bradd had reached his house, and was discussing the situation with his astonished spouse. She pooh-poohed the idea of the police and the medical faculty as being likely to cause complications with the owners, and, despite the remonstrances of her husband, insisted upon facing the mate alone.

"Now you go in the kitchen," she said, looking from the window. "Here he comes. You see how I'll settle him."

The skipper looked out of the window and saw the unhappy victim of Captain Zingall slowly approaching. His wife drew him away, and, despite his remonstrances, pushed him into the next room and closed the door.

She sat on the sofa calmly sewing, as the mate, whose hardihood was rapidly failing him, entered Her manner gave him no assistance whatever, and coming sheepishly in he took a chair.

"I've come home," he said at last

"So I see, Ben," said Mrs. Bradd, calmly.

"He's told her," said the mate to himself.

"Children all right?" he inquired, after another pause.

"Yes," said Mrs. Bradd, simply. "Little Joe's boots are almost off his feet, though."

"Ah," said the mate, blankly.

"I've been waiting for you to come, Ben," said Mrs. Bradd after a pause. "I want you to change a five-pound note Uncle Dick gave me."

"Can't do it," said the mate, briefly. The absence of Captain Bradd was disquieting to a bashful man in such a position, and he had looked forward to a stormy scene which was to bring him to his senses again.

"Show me what you've got," said Mrs. Bradd, leaning forward.

The mate pulled out an old leather purse and counted the contents, two pounds and a little silver.

"There isn't five pounds there," said Mrs. Bradd, "but I may as well take last week's housekeeping while you've got it out."

Before the mate could prevent her she had taken the two pounds and put it in her pocket. He looked at her placid face in amazement, but she met his gaze calmly and drummed on the table with her thimble.

"No, no, I want the money myself," said the mate at last. He put his hands to his head and began to prepare for the grand transformation scene. "My head's gone," he said, in a gurgling voice. "What am I doing here? Where am I?"

"Good gracious, what's the matter with the man?" said Mrs. Bradd, with a scream. She snatched up a bowl of flowers and flung the contents in his face as her husband burst into the room. The mate sprang to his feet, spluttering.

"What am I doing here, Cap'n Bradd?" he said in his usual voice.

"He's come round!" said Bradd, ecstatically. "He's come round. Oh, George, you have been playing the fool. Don't you know what you've been doing?"

The mate shook his head, and stared round the room. "I thought we were in London," he said, putting his hand to his head. "You said Cap'n Zingall was coming aboard. How did we get here? Where am I?"

In a hurried, breathless fashion the skipper told him, the mate regarding him the while with a stare of fixed incredulity.

"I can't understand it," he said at length. "My mind's a perfect blank."

"A perfect blank," said Mrs. Bradd, cheerfully. It might have been accident, but she tapped her pocket as she spoke, and the outwitted mate bit his lip as he realised his blunder, and turned to the door. The couple watched him as he slowly passed up the street.

"It's most extraordinary," said the skipper; "the most extraordinary case I ever heard of."

"So it is," said his wife, "and what's more extraordinary still for you, Ben, you're going to church on Sunday, and what's more extraordinary even than that, you are going to put two golden sovereigns in the plate."

BROTHER HUTCHINS

I've got a friend coming down with us this trip, George," said the master of the Wave, as they sat on deck after tea watching the river. "One of our new members, Brother Hutchins."

"From the Mission, I s'pose?" said the mate coldly.

"From the Mission," confirmed the skipper. "You'll like him, George; he's been one o' the greatest rascals that ever breathed."

"Well, I don't know what you mean," said the mate, looking up indignantly.

"He's 'ad a most interestin' life," said the skipper; "he's been in half the jails of England. To hear 'im talk is as good as reading a book. And 'e's as merry as they make 'em."

"Oh, and is 'e goin' to give us prayers afore breakfast like that fat-necked, white-faced old rascal what came down with us last summer and stole my boots?" demanded the mate.

"He never stole 'em, George," said the skipper.

"If you'd 'eard that man cry when I mentioned to 'im your unjust suspicions, you'd never have forgiven yourself. He told 'em at the meetin', an' they had prayers for you."

"You an' your Mission are a pack o' fools," said the mate scornfully. "You're always being done. A man comes to you an' ses 'e's found grace, and you find 'im a nice, easy, comfortable living. 'E sports a bit of blue ribbon and a red nose at the same time. Don't tell me. You ask me why I don't join you, and I tell you it's because I don't want to lose my commonsense."

"You'll know better one o' these days, George," said the skipper, rising. "I earnestly hope you'll 'ave some great sorrow or affliction, something almost too great for you to bear. It's the only thing that'll save you."

"I expect that fat chap what stole my boots would like to see it too," said the mate.

"He would," said the skipper solemnly. "He said so."

The mate got up, fuming and knocking his pipe out with great violence against the side of the schooner, stamped up and down the deck two or three times, and then, despairing of regaining his accustomed calm on board, went ashore.

It was late when he returned. A light burnt in the cabin, and the skipper with his spectacles on was reading aloud from an old number of the Evangelical Magazine to a thin, white-faced man dressed in black.

"That's my mate," said the skipper, looking up from his book.

"Is he one of our band?" inquired the stranger.

The skipper shook his head despondently.

"Not yet," said the stranger encouragingly.

"Seen too many of 'em," said the mate bluntly. "The more I see of 'em, the less I like 'em. It makes me feel wicked to look at 'em."

"Ah, that ain't you speaking now, it's the Evil One," said Mr. Hutchins confidently.

"I s'pose you know 'im pretty well," said the mate simply.

"I lived with him thirty years," said Mr. Hutchins solemnly, "then I got tired of him."

"I should think he got a bit sick too," said the mate. "Thirty days 'ud ha' been too long for me."

He went to his berth, to give Mr. Hutchins time to frame a suitable reply, and returned with a full bottle of whisky and a tumbler, and having drawn the cork with a refreshing pop, mixed himself a stiff glass and lit his pipe. Mr. Hutchins with a deep groan gazed reproachfully at the skipper and shook his head at the bottle.

"You know I don't like you to bring that filthy stuff in the cabin, George," said the skipper.

"It's not for me," said the mate flippantly. "It's for the Evil One. He ses the sight of his old pal 'Utchins 'as turned his stomach."

He glanced at the stranger and saw to his astonishment that he appeared to be struggling with a strong desire to laugh. His lips tightened and his shifty little eyes watered, but he conquered himself in a moment, and rising to his feet delivered a striking address in favour of teetotalism. He condemned whisky as not only wicked, but unnecessary, declaring with a side glance at the mate that two acidulated drops dissolved in water were an excellent substitute.

The sight of the whisky appeared to madden him, and the skipper sat spell-bound at his eloquence, until at length, after apostrophising the bottle in a sentence which left him breathless, he snatched it up and dashed it to pieces on the floor.

For a moment the mate was struck dumb with fury, then with a roar he leaped up and rushed for the lecturer, but the table was between them, and before he could get over it the skipper sprang up and seizing him by the arm, pushed his friend into the state-room.

"Lea' go," foamed the mate. "Let me get at him."

"George," said the skipper, still striving with him, "I'm ashamed of you."

"Ashamed be damned," yelled the mate, struggling. "What did he chuck my whisky away for?"

"He's a saint," said the skipper, relaxing his hold as he heard Mr. Hutchins lock himself in. "He's a saint, George. Seein' 'is beautiful words 'ad no effect on you, he 'ad recourse to strong measures."

"Wait till I get hold of 'im," said the mate menacingly. "Only wait, I'll saint 'im."

"Is he better, dear friend?" came the voice of Mr. Hutchins from beyond the door; "because I forgot the tumbler."

"Come out," roared the mate, "come out and upset it."

Mr. Hutchins declined the invitation, but from behind the door pleaded tearfully with the mate to lead a better life, and even rebuked the skipper for allowing the bottle of sin to be produced in the cabin. The skipper took the rebuke humbly; and after requesting Mr. Hutchins to sleep in the state-room that night in order to frustrate the evident designs of the mate, went on deck for a final look round and then came below and turned in himself.

The crew of the schooner were early astir next morning getting under way, but Mr. Hutchins kept his bed, although the mate slipped down to the cabin several times and tapped at his door. When he did come up the mate was at the wheel and the men down below getting breakfast.

"Sleep well?" inquired Mr. Hutchins softly, as he took a seat on the hatches, a little distance from him.

"I'll let you know when I haven't got this wheel," said the mate sourly.

"Do," said Mr. Hutchins genially. "We shall see you at our meeting to-night?" he asked blandly.

The mate disdained to reply, but his wrath when at Mr. Hutchins' request the cabin was invaded by the crew that evening, cannot be put into words.

For three nights they had what Mr. Hutchins described as love-feasts, and the mate as blamed bear-gardens. The crew were not particularly partial to hymns, considered as such, but hymns shouted out with the full force of their lungs while sharing the skipper's hymn-book appealed to them strongly. Besides, it maddened the mate, and to know that they were defying their superior, and at the same time doing good to their own souls, was very sweet The boy, whose voice was just breaking, got off some surprising effects, and seemed to compass about five octaves without distress.

When they were exhausted with singing Mr. Hutchins would give them a short address, generally choosing as his subject a strong, violent-tempered man given to drink and coarse language. The speaker proved conclusively that a man who drank would do other things in secret, and he pictured this man going home and beating his wife because she reproached him for breaking open the children's money-box to spend the savings on Irish whisky. At every point he made, he groaned, and the crew, as soon as they found they might groan too, did so with extraordinary gusto, the boy's groans being weird beyond conception.

They reached Plymouth, where they had to put out a few cases of goods, just in time to save the mate's reason, for the whole ship, owing to Mr. Hutchins' zeal, was topsy-turvy. The ship's cat sat up all one night cursing him and a blue ribbon he had tied round her neck, and even the battered old tea-pot came down to meals bedizened with bows of the same proselytising hue.

By the time they had got to their moorings it was too late to take the hatches off, and the crew sat gazing longingly at the lights ashore. Their delight when the visitor obtained permission for them to go ashore with him for a little stroll was unbounded, and they set off like schoolboys.

"They couldn't be with a better man," said the skipper, as the party moved off; "when I think of the good that man's done in under four days it makes me ashamed of myself."

"You'd better ship 'im as mate," said George. "There'd be a pair of you then."

"There's greater work for 'im to do," said the skipper solemnly.

He saw the mate's face in the waning light, and moved off with a sigh. The mate, for his part, leaned against the side smoking, and as the skipper declined to talk on any subject but Mr. Hutchins, relapsed into a moody silence until the return of the crew some two hours later.

"Mr. Hutchins is coming on after, sir," said the boy. "He told us to say he was paying a visit to a friend."

"What's the name of the pub?" asked the mate quietly.

"If you can't speak without showing your nasty temper, George, you'd better hold your tongue," said the skipper severely. "What's your opinion about Mr. Hutchins, my lads!"

"A more open 'arted man never breathed," said Dan, the oldest of the crew, warmly.

"Best feller I ever met in my life," said another.

"You hear that?" said the skipper.

"I hear," said the mate.

"'E's a Christian," said the boy. "I never knew what a Christian was before I met 'im. What do you think 'e give us?"

"Give you?" said the skipper.

"A pound cash," said the boy. "A golden sovring each. Tork about Christians! I wish I knew a few more of 'em."

"Well I never!" exclaimed the gratified skipper.

"An' the way 'e did it was so nice," said the oldest seaman. "'E ses, 'That's from me an' the skipper,' 'e ses. 'Thank the skipper for it as much as me,' 'e ses."

"Well now, don't waste it," said the skipper. "I should bank it if I was you. It'll make a nice little nest-egg."

"I 'ope it was come by honest, that's all," said the mate.

"O' course it was," cried the skipper. "You've got a 'ard, cruel 'art, George. P'raps if it 'ad been a little softer you'd 'ave 'ad one too."

"Blast 'is sovrings," said the surly mate. "I'd like to know where he got 'em from, an' wot e' means by saying it come from you as much as 'im. I never knew you to give money away."

"I s'pose," said the skipper very softly, "he means that I put such-like thoughts into 'is 'art. Well, you'd better turn in, my lads. We start work at four."

The hands went forward, and the skipper and mate descended to the cabin and prepared for sleep. The skipper set a lamp on the table ready for Mr. Hutchins when he should return, and after a short inward struggle bade the mate "good-night," and in a couple of minutes was fast asleep.

At four o'clock the mate woke suddenly to find the skipper standing by his berth. The lamp still stood burning on the table, fighting feebly against the daylight which was pouring in through the skylight.

"Not turned up yet?" said the mate, with a glance at the visitor's empty berth.

The skipper shook his head spiritlessly and pointed to the table. The mate following his finger, saw a small canvas bag, and by the side of it four-pence halfpenny in coppers and an unknown amount in brace buttons.

"There was twenty-three pounds freight money in that bag when we left London," said the skipper, finding his voice at last.

"Well, what do you think's become of it?" inquired the mate, taking up the lamp and blowing it out.

"I can't think," said the skipper, "my 'ed's all confused. Bro—Mr. Hutchins ain't come back yet."

"I s'pose he was late and didn't like to disturb you," said the mate without moving a muscle, "but I've no doubt 'e's all right. Don't you worry about him."

"It's very strange where it's gone, George," faltered the skipper, "very strange."

"Well, 'Utchins is a generous sort o' chap," said the mate, "'e give the men five pounds for nothing, so perhaps he'll give you something—when 'e comes back."

"Go an' ask the crew to come down here," said the skipper, sinking on a locker and gazing at the brazen collection before him.

The mate obeyed, and a few minutes afterwards returned with the men, who, swarming into the cabin, listened sympathetically as the skipper related his loss.

"It's a mystery which nobody can understand, sir," said old Dan when he had finished, "and it's no use tryin'."

"One o' them things what won't never be cleared up properly," said the cook comfortably.

"Well, I don't like to say it," said the skipper, "but I must. The only man who could have taken it was Hutchins."

"Wot, sir," said Dan, "that blessed man! Why, I'd laugh at the idea."

"He couldn't do it," said the boy, "not if he tried he couldn't. He was too good."

"He's taken that twenty-three poun'," said the skipper deliberately; "eighteen, we'll call it, because I'm goin' to have five of it back."

"You're labourin' under a great mistake, sir," said Dan ambiguously.

"Are you going to give me that money?" said the skipper loudly.

"Beggin' your pardon, sir, no," said the cook, speaking for the rest, as he put his foot on the companion-ladder. "Brother 'Utchins gave us that money for singing them 'ims so well. 'E said so, and we ain't 'ad no call to think as it warn't honestly come by. Nothing could ever make us think that, would it, mates?"

"Nothing," said the others with exemplary firmness. "It couldn't be done."

They followed the cook up on deck, and leaning over the side, gazed in a yearning fashion toward the place where they had last seen their benefactor. Then with a sorrowful presentiment that they would never look upon his like again, they turned away and prepared for the labours of the day.

THE BULLY OF THE "CAVENDISH"

Talking of prize-fighters, sir," said the night-watchman, who had nearly danced himself over the edge of the wharf in illustrating one of Mr. Corbett's most trusted blows, and was now sitting down taking in sufficient air for three, "they ain't wot they used to be when I was a boy. They advertise in the papers for months and months about their fights, and when it does come off, they do it with gloves, and they're all right agin a day or two arter.

"I saw a picter the other day o' one punching a bag wot couldn't punch back, for practice. Why, I remember as a young man Sinker Pitt, as used to 'ave the King's Arms 'ere in 'is old age; when 'e wanted practice 'is plan was to dress up in a soft 'at and black coat like a chapel minister or something, and go in a pub and contradict people; sailor-men for choice. He'd ha' no more thought o' hitting a pore 'armless bag than I should ha' thought of hitting 'im.

"The strangest prize-fighter I ever come acrost was one wot shipped with me on the Cavendish. He was the most eggstrordinary fighter I've ever seen or 'eard of, and 'e got to be such a nuisance afore 'e'd done with us that we could 'ardly call our souls our own. He shipped as an ordinary seaman—a unfair thing to do, as 'e was anything but ordinary, and 'ad no right to be there at all.

"We'd got one terror on board afore he come, and that was Bill Bone, one o' the biggest and strongest men I've ever seen down a ship's fo'c's'le, and that's saying a good deal. Built more like a bull than a man, 'e was, and when he was in his tantrums the best thing to do was to get out of 'is way or else get into your bunk and keep quiet. Oppersition used to send 'im crazy a'most, an' if 'e said a red shirt was a blue one, you 'ad to keep quiet. It didn't do to agree with 'im and call it blue even, cos if you did he'd call you a liar and punch you for telling lies.

"He was the only drawback to that ship. We 'ad a nice old man, good mates, and good grub. You may know it was A1 when I tell you that most of us 'ad been in 'er for several v'y'ges.

"But Bill was a drawback, and no mistake. In the main he was a 'earty, good-tempered sort o' shipmate as you'd wish to see, only, as I said afore, oppersition was a thing he could not and would not stand. It used to fly to his 'ed direckly.

"The v'y'ge I'm speaking of—we used to trade between Australia and London—Bill came aboard about an hour afore the ship sailed. The rest of us was already aboard and down below, some of us stowing our things away and the rest sitting down and telling each other lies about wot we'd been doing. Bill came lurching down the ladder, and Tom Baker put 'is 'and to 'im to steady 'im as he got to the bottom.

"'Who are you putting your 'ands on?' ses Bill, glaring at 'im.

"'Only 'olding you up, Bill,' ses Tom, smiling.

"'Oh,' ses Bill.

"He put 'is back up agin a bunk and pulled his-self together.

"''Olding of me—up—was you?' he ses; 'whaffor, if I might be so bold as to arsk?'

"'I thought your foot 'ad slipped, Bill, old man,' ses Tom; 'but I'm sorry if it 'adn't.'

"Bill looks at 'im agin, 'ard.

"'Sorry if my foot didn't slip?' he ses.

"'You know wot I mean, Bill,' ses Tom, smiling a uneasy smile.

"'Don't laugh at me,' roars Bill.

"'I wasn't laughing, Bill, old pal,' ses Tom.

"''E's called me a liar,' ses Bill, looking round at us; 'called me a liar. 'Old my coat, Charlie, and I'll split 'im in halves.'

"Charlie took the coat like a lamb, though he was Tom's pal, and Tom looked round to see whether he couldn't nip up the ladder and get away, but Bill was just in front of it. Then Tom found out that one of 'is bootlaces was undone and he knelt down to do it up, and this young ordinary seaman, Joe Simms by name, put his 'ead out of his bunk and he ses, quiet-like:

"'You ain't afraid of that thing, mate, are you?'

"'Wot?' screams Bill, starting.

"'Don't make such a noise when I'm speaking,' ses Joe; 'where's your manners, you great 'ulking rascal?'

"I thought Bill would ha' dropped with surprise at being spoke to like that. His face was purple all over and 'e stood staring at Joe as though 'e didn't know wot to make of 'im. And we stared too, Joe being a smallish sort o' chap and not looking at all strong.

"'Go easy, mate,' whispers Tom; 'you don't know who you're talking to.'

"'Bosh,' ses Joe, 'he's no good. He's too fat and too silly to do any 'arm. He sha'n't 'urt you while I'm 'ere.'

"He just rolled out of 'is bunk and, standing in front of Bill, put 'is fists up at 'im and stared 'im straight in the eye.

"'You touch that man,' he ses, quietly, pointing to Tom, 'and I'll give you such a dressing-down as you've never 'ad afore. Mark my words, now.'

"'I wasn't going to 'it him,' ses Bill, in a strange, mild voice.

"'You'd better not,' ses the young 'un, shaking his fist at 'im; 'you'd better not, my lad. If there's any fighting to be done in this fo'c's'le I'll do it. Mind that.'

"It's no good me saying we was staggered; becos staggered ain't no word for it. To see Bill put 'is hands in 'is pockets and try and whistle, and then sit down on a locker and scratch 'is head, was the most amazing thing I've ever seen. Presently 'e begins to sing under his breath.

"'Stop that 'umming,' ses Joe; 'when I want you to 'um, I'll tell you.'

"Bill left off 'umming, and then he gives a little cough behind the back of 'is 'and, and, arter fidgeting about a bit with 'is feet, went up on deck again.

"'Strewth,' ses Tom, looking round at us, "'ave we shipped a bloomin' prize-fighter?'

"'Wot did you call me?' ses Joe, looking at 'im.

"'Nothing, mate,' ses Tom, drawing back.

"'You keep a quiet tongue in your 'ed,' ses Joe, 'and speak when you're spoken to, my lad.'

"He was a ordinary seaman, mind, talking to A. B.'s like that. Men who'd been up aloft and doing their little bit when 'e was going about catching cold in 'is little petticuts. Still, if Bill could stand it, we supposed as we'd better.

"Bill stayed up on deck till we was under way, and 'is spirit seemed to be broke. He went about 'is work like a man wot was walking in 'is sleep, and when breakfast come 'e 'ardly tasted it.

"Joe made a splendid breakfast, and when he'd finished 'e went to Bill's bunk and chucked the things out all over the place and said 'e was going to 'ave it for himself. And Bill sat there and took it all quiet, and by-and-by he took 'is things up and put them in Joe's bunk without a word.

"It was the most peaceful fust day we 'ad ever 'ad down that fo'c's'le, Bill usually being in 'is tantrums the fust day or two at sea, and wanting to know why 'e'd been born. If you talked you was noisy and worriting, and if you didn't talk you was sulky; but this time 'e sat quite still and didn't interfere a bit. It was such a pleasant change that we all felt a bit grateful, and at tea-time Tom Baker patted Joe on the back and said he was one o' the right old sort.

"'You've been in a scrape or two in your time, I know,' he ses, admiring like. 'I knew you was a bit of a one with your fists direckly I see you.'

"'Oh, 'ow's that?' asks Joe.

"'I could see by your nose,' ses Tom.

"You never know how to take people like that. The words 'ad 'ardly left Tom's lips afore the other ups with a basin of 'ot tea and heaves it all over 'im.

"'Take that, you insulting rascal,' he ses, as Tom jumped up spluttering and wiping 'is face with his coat. 'How dare you insult me?'

"'Get up,' ses Tom, dancing with rage. 'Get up; prize-fighter or no prize-fighter, I'll mark you.'

"'Sit down,' ses Bill, turning round.

"I'm going to 'ave a go at 'im, Bill,' ses Tom; 'if you're afraid of 'im, I ain't.'

"'Sit down,' ses Bill, starting up. ''Ow dare you insult me like that?'

"'Like wot?' ses Tom, staring.

"'If I can't lick 'im you can't,' ses Bill; 'that's 'ow it is, mate.'

"'But I can try,' ses Tom.

"'All right,' ses Bill. 'Me fust, then if you lick me, you can 'ave a go at 'im. If you can't lick me, 'ow can you lick 'im?'

"'Sit down, both of you,' ses young Joe, drinking Bill's tea to make up for 'is own. 'And mind you, I'm cock o' this fo'c's'le, and don't you forget it. Sit down, both of you, afore I start on you.'

"They both sat down, but Tom wasn't quick enough to please Bill, and he got a wipe o' the side o' the 'ead that made it ring for an hour afterwards.

"That was the beginning of it, and instead of 'aving one master we found we'd got two, owing to the eggstrordinry way Bill had o' looking at things. He gave Joe best without even 'aving a try at him, and if anybody else wanted to 'ave a try, it was a insult to Bill. We couldn't make 'ed or tail of it, and all we could get out of Bill was that 'e had one time 'ad a turn-up with Joe Simms ashore, which he'd remember all 'is life. It must ha' been something of a turn, too, the way Bill used to try and curry favour with 'im.

"In about three days our life wasn't worth living, and the fo'c's'le was more like a Sunday-school class than anything else. In the fust place Joe put down swearing. He wouldn't 'ave no bad langwidge, he said, and he didn't neither. If a man used a bad word Joe would pull 'im up the fust time, and the second he'd order Bill to 'it 'im, being afraid of 'urting 'im too much 'imself. 'Arf the men 'ad to leave off talking altogether when Joe was by, but the way they used to swear when he wasn't was something shocking. Harry Moore got clergyman's sore throat one arternoon through it.

"Then Joe objected to us playing cards for money, and we 'ad to arrange on the quiet that brace buttons was ha'-pennies and coat buttons pennies, and that lasted until one evening Tom Baker got up and danced and nearly went off 'is 'ead with joy through havin' won a few dozen. That was enough for Joe, and Bill by his orders took the cards and pitched 'em over the side.

"Sweet-'earting and that sort o' thing Joe couldn't abear, and Ned Davis put his foot into it finely one arternoon through not knowing. He was lying in 'is bunk smoking and thinking, and by and by he looked across at Bill, who was 'arf asleep, and 'e ses:

"'I wonder whether you'll see that little gal at Melbourne agin this trip, Bill.'

"Bill's eyes opened wide and he shook 'is fist at Ned, as Ned thought, playful-like.

"'All right, I'm a-looking at you, Bill,' 'e ses. 'I can see you.'

"'What gal is that, Ned?' ses Joe, who was in the next bunk to him, and I saw Bill's eyes screw up tight, and 'e suddenly fell fast asleep.

"'I don't know 'er name,' ses Ned, 'but she was very much struck on Bill; they used to go to the theayter together.'

"Pretty gal?' ses Joe, leading 'im on.

"'Rather,' ses Ned. Trust Bill for that, 'e. always gets the prettiest gal in the place—I've known as many as six and seven to—'

"'WOT!' screams Bill, waking up out of 'is sleep, and jumping out of 'is bunk.

"'Keep still, Bill, and don't interfere when I'm talking,' ses Joe, very sharp.

"''E's insulted me,' ses Bill; 'talking about gals when everybody knows I 'ate 'em worse than pison.'

"'Hold your tongue,' ses Joe. 'Now, Ned, what's this about this little gal? What's 'er name?'

"'It was only a little joke o' mine,' ses Ned, who saw 'e'd put 'is foot in it. 'Bill 'ates 'em worse than—worse than—pison.'

"'You're telling me a lie,' ses Joe, sternly. 'Who was it?'

"'It was only my fun, Joe,' ses Ned.

"'Oh, very well then. I'm going to 'ave a bit of fun now,' ses Joe. 'Bill!'

"'Yes,' ses Bill.

"'I won't 'it Ned myself for fear I shall do 'im a lasting injury,' ses Joe, 'so you just start on 'im and keep on till 'e tells all about your goings on with that gal.'

"'Hit 'im to make 'im tell about me? ses Bill, staring 'is 'ardest.

"'You 'eard wot I said,' ses Joe; 'don't repeat my words. You a married man, too; I've got sisters of my own, and I'm going to put this sort o' thing down. If you don't down 'im, I will.'

"Ned wasn't much of a fighter, and I 'alf expected to see 'im do a bolt up on deck and complain to the skipper. He did look like it for a moment, then he stood up, looking a bit white as Bill walked over to 'im, and the next moment 'is fist flew out, and afore we could turn round I'm blest if Bill wasn't on the floor. 'E got up as if 'e was dazed like, struck out wild at Ned and missed 'im, and the next moment was knocked down agin. We could 'ardly believe our eyes, and as for Ned, 'e looked as though 'e'd been doing miracles by mistake.

"When Bill got up the second time 'e was that shaky 'e could 'ardly stand, and Ned 'ad it all 'is own way, until at last 'e got Bill's 'ead under 'is arm and punched at it till they was both tired.

"'All right,' ses Bill; 'I've 'ad enough. I've met my master.'

"'Wot?' ses Joe, staring.

"'I've met my master,' ses Bill, going and sitting down. 'Ned 'as knocked me about crool.'

"Joe looked at 'im, speechless, and then without saying another word, or 'aving a go at Ned himself, as we expected, 'e went up on deck, and Ned crossed over and sat down by Bill.

"'I 'ope I didn't hurt you, mate,' he ses, kindly.

"'Hurt me?' roars Bill. 'You! You 'urt me? You, you little bag o' bones. Wait till I get you ashore by yourself for five minits, Ned Davis, and then you'll know what 'urting means.'

"'I don't understand you, Bill,' ses Ned; 'you're a mystery, that's what you are; but I tell you plain when you go ashore you don't have me for a companion.'

"It was a mystery to all of us, and it got worse and worse as time went on. Bill didn't dare to call 'is soul 'is own, although Joe only hit 'im once the whole time, and then not very hard, and he excused 'is cowardice by telling us of a man Joe 'ad killed in a fight down in one o' them West-end clubs.

"Wot with Joe's Sunday-school ways and Bill backing 'em up, we was all pretty glad by the time we got to Melbourne. It was like getting out o' pris'n to get away from Joe for a little while. All but Bill, that is, and Joe took 'im to hear a dissolving views on John Bunyan. Bill said 'e'd be delighted to go, but the language he used about 'im on the quiet when he came back showed what 'e thought of it. I don't know who John Bunyan is, or wot he's done, but the things Bill said about 'im I wouldn't soil my tongue by repeating.

"Arter we'd been there two or three days we began to feel a'most sorry, for Bill. Night arter night, when we was ashore, Joe would take 'im off and look arter 'im, and at last, partly for 'is sake, but more to see the fun, Tom Baker managed to think o' something to put things straight.

"'You stay aboard to-night, Bill,' he ses one morning, 'and you'll see something that 'll startle you.'

"'Worse than you?' ses Bill, whose temper was getting worse and worse.

"'There'll be an end o' that bullying, Joe,' ses Tom, taking 'im by the arm. 'We've arranged to give 'im a lesson as'll lay 'im up for a time.'

"'Oh,' ses Bill, looking 'ard at a boat wot was passing.

"'We've got Dodgy Pete coming to see us tonight,' ses Tom, in a whisper; 'there'll only be the second officer aboard, and he'll likely be asleep. Dodgy's one o' the best light-weights in Australia, and if 'e don't fix up Mister Joe, it'll be a pity.'

"'You're a fair treat, Tom,' ses Bill, turning round; 'that's what you are. A fair treat.'

"'I thought you'd be pleased, Bill,' ses Tom.

"Pleased ain't no name for it, Tom,' answers Bill. 'You've took a load off my mind.'

"The fo'c's'le was pretty full that evening, everybody giving each other a little grin on the quiet, and looking over to where Joe was sitting in 'is bunk putting a button or two on his coat. At about ha'-past six Dodgy comes aboard, and the fun begins to commence.

"He was a nasty, low-looking little chap, was Dodgy, very fly-looking and very conceited. I didn't like the look of 'im at all, and unbearable as Joe was, it didn't seem to be quite the sort o' thing to get a chap aboard to 'ammer a shipmate you couldn't 'ammer yourself.

"'Nasty stuffy place you've got down 'ere,' ses Dodgy, who was smoking a big cigar; 'I can't think 'ow you can stick it.'

"'It ain't bad for a fo'c's'le,' ses Charlie.

"'An' what's that in that bunk over there?' ses Dodgy, pointing with 'is cigar at Joe.

"'Hush, be careful,' ses Tom, with a wink; 'that's a prize-fighter.'

"'Oh,' ses Dodgy, grinning, 'I thought it was a monkey.'

"You might 'ave heard a pin drop, and there was a pleasant feeling went all over us at the thought of the little fight we was going to see all to ourselves, as Joe lays down the jacket he was stitching at and just puts 'is little 'ead over the side o' the bunk.

"'Bill,' he ses, yawning.

"'Well,' ses Bill, all on the grin like the rest of us.

"'Who is that 'andsome, gentlemanly-looking young feller over there smoking a half-crown cigar?' ses Joe.

"That's a young gent wot's come down to 'ave a look round,' ses Tom, as Dodgy takes 'is cigar out of 'is mouth and looks round, puzzled.

"'Wot a terror 'e must be to the gals, with them lovely little peepers of 'is,' ses Joe, shaking 'is 'ead. 'Bill!'

"'Well,' ses Bill, agin, as Dodgy got up.

"'Take that lovely little gentleman and kick 'im up the fo'c's'le ladder,' ses Joe, taking up 'is jacket agin; 'and don't make too much noise over it, cos I've got a bit of a 'ead-ache, else I'd do it myself.'

"There was a laugh went all round then, and Tom Baker was near killing himself, and then I'm blessed if Bill didn't get up and begin taking off 'is coat.

"'Wot's the game?' ses Dodgy, staring.

"'I'm obeying orders,' ses Bill. 'Last time I was in London, Joe 'ere half killed me one time, and 'e made me promise to do as 'e told me for six months. I'm very sorry, mate, but I've got to kick you up that ladder.'

"'You kick me up?' ses Dodgy, with a nasty little laugh.

"'I can try, mate, can't I?' ses Bill, folding 'is things up very neat and putting 'em on a locker.

"''Old my cigar,' ses Dodgy, taking it out of 'is mouth and sticking it in Charlie's. 'I don't need to take my coat off to 'im.'

"'E altered 'is mind, though, when he saw Bill's chest and arms, and not only took off his coat, but his waistcoat too. Then, with a nasty look at Bill, 'e put up 'is fists and just pranced up to 'im.

"The fust blow Bill missed, and the next moment 'e got a tap on the jaw that nearly broke it, and that was followed up by one in the eye that sent 'im staggering up agin the side, and when 'e was there Dodgy's fists were rattling all round 'im.

"I believe it was that that brought Bill round, and the next moment Dodgy was on 'is back with a blow that nearly knocked his 'ead off. Charlie grabbed at Tom's watch and began to count, and after a little bit called out Time,' It was a silly thing to do, as it would 'ave stopped the fight then and there if it 'adn't been for Tom's presence of mind, saying it was two minutes slow. That gave Dodgy a chance, and he got up again and walked round Bill very careful, swearing 'ard at the small size of the fo'c's'le.

"He got in three or four at Bill afore you could wink a'most, and when Bill 'it back 'e wasn't there. That seemed to annoy Bill more than anything, and he suddenly flung out 'is arms, and grabbing 'old of 'im flung 'im right across the fo'c's'le to where, fortunately for 'im—Dodgy, I mean—Tom Baker was sitting.

"Charlie called Time' again, and we let 'em 'ave five minutes while we 'elped Tom to bed, and then wot 'e called the 'disgusting exhibishun' was resoomed. Bill 'ad dipped 'is face in a bucket and 'ad rubbed 'is great arms all over and was as fresh as a daisy. Dodgy looked a bit tottery, but 'e was game all through and very careful, and, try as Bill might, he didn't seem to be able to get 'old of 'im agin.

"In five minutes more, though, it was all over, Dodgy not being able to see plain—except to get out o' Bill's way—and hitting wild. He seemed to think the whole fo'c's'le was full o' Bills sitting on a locker and waiting to be punched, and the end of it was a knock-out blow from the real Bill which left 'im on the floor without a soul offering to pick 'im up.

"Bill 'elped 'im up at last and shook hands with 'im, and they rinsed their faces in the same bucket, and began to praise each other up. They sat there purring like a couple o' cats, until at last we 'eard a smothered voice coming from Joe Simms's bunk.

"'Is it all over?' he asks.

"'Yes,' ses somebody.

"'How is Bill?' ses Joe's voice again.

"'Look for yourself,' ses Tom.

"Joe sat up in 'is bunk then and looked out, and he no sooner saw Bill's face than he gave a loud cry and fell back agin, and, as true as I'm sitting here, fainted clean away. We was struck all of a 'eap, and then Bill picked up the bucket and threw some water over 'im, and by and by he comes round agin and in a dazed sort o' way puts his arm round Bill's neck and begins to cry.

"'Mighty Moses!' ses Dodgy Pete, jumping up, 'it's a woman!'

"'It's my wife!' ses Bill.

"We understood it all then, leastways the married ones among us did. She'd shipped aboard partly to be with Bill and partly to keep an eye on 'im, and Tom Baker's mistake about a prizefighter had just suited her book better than anything. How Bill was to get 'er home 'e couldn't think, but it 'appened the second officer had been peeping down the fo'c's'le, waiting for ever so long for a suitable opportunity to stop the fight, and the old man was so tickled about the way we'd all been done 'e gave 'er a passage back as stewardess to look arter the ship's cat."

THE CABIN PASSENGER

The captain of the Fearless came on to the wharf in a manner more suggestive of deer-stalking than that of a prosaic shipmaster returning to his craft. He dodged round an empty van, lurked behind an empty barrel, flitted from that to a post, and finally from the interior of a steam crane peeped melodramatically on to the deck of his craft.

To the ordinary observer there was no cause for alarm. The decks were a bit slippery but not dangerous except to a novice; the hatches were on, and in the lighted galley the cook might be discovered moving about in a manner indicative of quiet security and an untroubled conscience.

With a last glance behind him the skipper descended from the crane and stepped lightly aboard.

"Hist," said the cook, coming out quietly. "I've been watching for you to come."

"Damned fine idea of watching you've got," said the skipper irritably. "What is it?"

The cook jerked his thumb towards the cabin. "He's down there," he said in a hoarse whisper. "The mate said when you came aboard you was just to go and stand near the companion and whistle 'God Save the Queen' and he'll come up to you to see what's to be done."

"Whistle!" said the skipper, trying to moisten his parched lips with his tongue. "I couldn't whistle just now to save my life."

"The mate don't know what to do, and that was to be the signal," said the cook. "He's darn there with him givin' 'im drink and amoosin' 'im."

"Well, you go and whistle it," said the skipper.

The cook wiped his mouth on the back of his hand. "'Ow does it go?" he inquired anxiously. "I never could remember toons."

"Oh, go and tell Bill to do it!" said the skipper impatiently.

Summoned noiselessly by the cook, Bill came up from the forecastle, and on learning what was required of him pursed up his lips and started our noble anthem with a whistle of such richness and volume that the horrified skipper was almost deafened with it. It acted on the mate like a charm, and he came from below and closed Bill's mouth, none too gently, with a hand which shook with excitement. Then, as quietly as possible, he closed the companion and secured the fastenings.

"He's all right," he said to the skipper breathlessly. "He's a prisoner. He's 'ad four goes o' whisky, an' he seems inclined to sleep."

"Who let him go down the cabin?" demanded the skipper angrily. "It's a fine thing I can't leave the ship for an hour or so but what I come back and find people sitting all round my cabin."

"He let hisself darn," said the cook, who saw a slight opening advantageous to himself in connection with a dish smashed the day before, "an' I was that surprised, not to say alarmed, that I dropped the large dish and smashed it."

"What did he say?" inquired the skipper.

"The blue one, I mean," said the cook, who wanted that matter settled for good, "the one with the place at the end for the gravy to run into."

"What did he say?" vociferated the skipper.

"'E ses, 'Ullo,' he ses, 'you've done it now, old man,'" replied the truthful cook.

The skipper turned a furious face to the mate.

"When the cook come up and told me," said the mate, in answer, "I see at once what was up, so I went down and just talked to him clever like."

"I should like to know what you said," muttered the skipper.

"Well, if you think you can do better than I did you'd better go down and see him," retorted the mate hotly. "After all, it's you what 'e come to see. He's your visitor."

"No offence, Bob," said the skipper. "I didn't mean nothing."

"I don't know nothin' o' horse-racin'," continued the mate, with an insufferable air, "and I never 'ad no money troubles in my life, bein' always brought up proper at 'ome and warned of what would 'appen, but I know a sheriff's officer when I see 'im."

"What am I to do?" groaned the skipper, too depressed even to resent his subordinate's manner. "It's a judgment summons. It's ruin if he gets me."

"Well, so far as I can see, the only thing for you to do is to miss the ship this trip," said the mate, without looking at him. "I can take her out all right."

"I won't," said the skipper, interrupting fiercely.

"Very well, you'll be nabbed," said the mate.

"You've been wanting to handle this craft a long time," said the skipper fiercely. "You could ha' got rid of him if you'd wanted to. He's no business down my cabin."

"I tried everything I could think of," asseverated the mate.

"Well, he's come down on my ship without being asked," said the skipper fiercely, "and, damme, he can stay there. Cast off."

"But," said the mate, "s'pose—"

"Cast off," repeated the skipper. "He's come on my ship, and I'll give him a trip free."

"And where are you and the mate to sleep?" inquired the cook, who was a man of pessimistic turn of mind, and given to forebodings.

"In your bunks," said the skipper brutally. "Cast off there."

The men obeyed, grinning, and the schooner was soon threading her way in the darkness down the river, the skipper listening somewhat nervously for the first intimation of his captive's awakening.

He listened in vain that night, for the prisoner made no sign, but at six o'clock in the morning, when the Fearless, coming within sight of the Nore, began to dance like a cork upon the waters, the mate reported hollow groans from the cabin.

"Let him groan," said the skipper briefly, "as holler as he likes."

"Well, I'll just go down and see how he is," said the mate.

"You stay where you are," said the skipper sharply.

"Well, but you ain't going to starve the man?"

"Nothing to do with me," said the skipper ferociously; "if a man likes to come down and stay in my cabin, that's his business. I'm not supposed to know he's there; and if I like to lock my cabin up and sleep in a foc'sle what's got more fleas in it than ten other foc'sles put together, and what smells worse than ten foc'sles rolled into one, that's my business."

"Yes, but I don't want to berth for'ard too," grumbled the other. "He can't touch me. I can go and sleep in my berth."

"You'll do what I wish, my lad," said the skipper.

"I'm the mate," said the other darkly.

"And I'm the master," said the other; "if the master of a ship can stay down the foc'sle, I'm sure a tuppeny-ha'penny mate can."

"The men don't like it," objected the mate.

"Damn the men," said the skipper politely, "and as to starving the chap, there's a water-bottle full o' water in my state-room, to say nothing of a jug, and a bag o' biscuits under the table."

The mate walked off whistling, and the skipper, by no means so easy in his mind as he pretended to be, began to consider ways and means out of the difficulty which he foresaw must occur when they reached port.

"What sort o' looking chap is he?" he inquired of the cook.

"Big, strong-looking chap," was the reply.

"Look as though he'd make a fuss if I sent you and Bill down below to gag him when we get to the other end?" suggested the skipper.

The cook said that judging by appearances "fuss" would be no word for it.

"I can't understand him keeping so quiet," said the skipper; "that's what gets over me."

"He's biding 'is time, I expect," said the cook comfortingly. "He's a 'ard looking customer, 'sides which he's likely sea-sick."

The day passed slowly, and as night approached a sense of mystery and discomfort overhung the vessel. The man at the wheel got nervous, and flattered Bill into keeping him company by asking him to spin him a yarn. He had good reason for believing that he knew his comrade's stock of stories by heart, but in the sequel it transpired that there was one, of a prisoner turning into a cat and getting out of the porthole and running up helmsmen's backs, which he hadn't heard before. And he told Bill in the most effective language he could command that he never wanted to hear it again.

The night passed and day broke, and still the mysterious passenger made no sign. The crew got in the habit of listening at the companion and peeping through the skylight; but the door of the stateroom was closed, and the cabin itself as silent as the grave. The skipper went about with a troubled face, and that afternoon, unable to endure the suspense any longer, civilly asked the mate to go below and investigate.

"I'd rather not," said the mate, shrugging his shoulders.

"I'd sooner he served me and have done with it," said the skipper. "I get thinking all sorts of awful things."

"Well, why don't you go down yourself?" said the mate. "He'd serve you fast enough, I've no doubt."

"Well, it may be just his artfulness," said the skipper; "an' I don't want to humour him if he's all right. I'm askin' it as a favour, Bob."

"I'll go if the cook'll come," said the mate after a pause.

The cook hesitated.

"Go on, cook," said the skipper sharply; "don't keep the mate waiting, and, whatever you do, don't let him come up on deck."

The mate led the way to the companion, and, opening it quietly, led the way below, followed by the cook. There was a minute's awful suspense, and then a wild cry rang out below, and the couple came dashing madly up on deck again.

"What is it?" inquired the pallid skipper.

The mate, leaning for support against the wheel, opened his mouth, but no words came; the cook, his hands straight by his side and his eyes glassy, made a picture from which the crew drew back in awe.

"What's—the—matter?" said the skipper again.

Then the mate, regaining his composure by an effort, spoke.

"You needn't trouble to fasten the companion again," he said slowly.

The skipper's face changed from white to grey. "Why not?" he asked in a trembling voice.

"He's dead," was the solemn reply.

"Nonsense," said the other, with quivering lips. "He's shamming or else fainting. Did you try to bring him round?"

"I did not," said the mate. "I don't deceive you. I didn't stay down there to do no restoring, and I don't think you would either."

"Go down and see whether you can wake him, cook," said the skipper.

"Not me," said the cook with a mighty shudder.

Two of the hands went and peeped furtively down through the skylight. The empty cabin looked strangely quiet and drear, and the door of the stateroom stood ajar. There was nothing to satisfy their curiosity, but they came back looking as though they had seen a ghost.

"What's to be done?" said the skipper helplessly.

"Nothing can be done," said the mate. "He's beyond our aid."

"I wasn't thinking about him," said the skipper.

"Well, the best thing you can do when we get to Plymouth is to bolt," said the mate. "We'll hide it up as long as we can to give you a start It's a hanging matter."

The hapless master of the Fearless wiped his clammy brow. "I can't think he's dead," he said slowly. "Who'll come down with me to see?"

"You'd better leave it alone," said the mate kindly, "it ain't pleasant, and besides that we can all swear up to the present that you haven't touched him or been near him."

"Who'll come down with me?" repeated the skipper. "I believe it's a trick, and that he'll start up and serve me, but I feel I must go."

He caught Bill's eye, and that worthy seaman, after a short tussle with his nerves, shuffled after him. The skipper, brushing aside the mate, who sought to detain him, descended first, and entering the cabin stood hesitating, with Bill close behind him.

"Just open the door, Bill," he said slowly.

"Arter you, sir," said the well-bred Bill.

The skipper stepped slowly towards it and flung it suddenly open. Then he drew back with a sharp cry and looked nervously about him. The bed was empty.

"Where's he gone?" whispered the trembling Bill.

The other made no reply, but in a dazed fashion began to grope about the cabin. It was a small place and soon searched, and the two men sat down and eyed each other in blank amazement.

"Where is he?" said Bill at length.

The skipper shook his head helplessly, and was about to ascribe the mystery to supernatural agencies when the truth in all its naked simplicity flashed upon him and he spoke. "It's the mate," he said slowly, "the mate and the cook. I see it all now; there's never been anybody here. It was a little job on the mate's part to get the ship. If you want to hear a couple o' rascals sized up, Bill, come on deck."

And Bill, grinning in anticipation, went.

W.W. Jacobs – A Short Biography

William Wymark Jacobs was born on September 8, 1863 in the Wapping district of London, England. An author, humorist and dramatist, Jacobs is best remembered for the enduring classic tale of horror - "The Monkey's Paw".

As a youth, Jacobs grew up near the Wapping docks in London, where his father was a wharf manager. The family's first home was home was a house on a River Thames wharf.

The docklands setting would show up frequently in his later literary output. Jacobs, the wharf rat, and his three siblings lost their mother when they were all still young children. Their father, William Gage Jacobs, remarried and fathered a further seven children with his erstwhile housekeeper Ellen Florey. Although he grew up surrounded by poverty, Jacobs himself received a formal education in London, first at a private prep school and later at the Birkbeck Literary and Scientific Institute (now part of the University of London and known as Birkbeck College).

Jacobs' adult working life began with a clerical position at the Post Office Savings Bank. The job was not a stimulating one but Jacobs put his imagination to good use and started to write short stories, sketches and articles, many of which appeared in the Post Office house publication "Blackfriars Magazine."

Although Jacobs did receive his fair share of rejection slips at the beginning of his career, many works written during this period of clerical employment appeared in the "Idler" and "Today" magazines, both of which were edited by noted humorist Jerome K. Jerome, who had taken a liking to Jacobs' stories.

From 1898, Jacobs also published stories in "The Strand", a popular, monthly fiction and general interest magazine. The arrangement stayed in place for most of his life and many of the works in Jacobs' subsequent collections – including the nautical serialization A Master of Craft (1899-1900) - appeared there first.

Jacobs' first volume of collected works was published in 1896. Many Cargoes, a selection of sea-faring yarns, established Jacobs as a popular writer and humorist with a penchant for authentic dialogue and trick endings (critics of the day referred to him as the "O. Henry of the Waterfront").

A year later he published a novelette, The Skipper's Wooing, and in 1898 and another collection of short stories titled Sea Urchins. These works painted vivid, if imaginatively stretched, pictures of dockland and seafaring London with colourful characters (such as "The Night Watchman", Ginger Dick) that now seem archetypal.

Many of Jacobs' periodical publications and first editions were illustrated with woodcuts and ink drawings, as was still the custom at the turn of the 20th century. The author worked regularly with artists such as E.W. Kemble, who had illustrated Mark Twain's Adventures of Huckleberry Finn and Harriet Beecher Stowe's Uncle Tom's Cabin, and his good friend Will Owen, who eventually became a household name on the strength of his iconic Bisto Kids, Bovril and Lux Soap advertising posters.

By 1899, Jacobs was able to quit the post office and finally begin a career making a living as a full-time writer.

He married the noted suffragist Agnes Eleanor Williams (who had been jailed for her protest activities) in 1900. They set up a household in Loughton, Essex as well as living part of the year in central London. The couple went on to have five children together though their marriage was considered an unhappy one.

The publication of two short novels: At Sunwich Port (a romantic tale of rival sea captains in the fictional seaside community of Sunwich standing in for the actual East England community of Sandwich, Kent) and Dialstone Lane (another small town romance involving intrigue and buried treasure), in 1902 and 1904 respectively, cemented Jacobs' reputation as one of the leading British authors of the new century.

On the foundations of a continuing ability to write for his audience he was readily published though he never strayed too far from what was becoming his familiar, dependable style. There followed a string of further successful publications, including Captain's All (1905), Night Watches (1914), The Castaways (1916), and Sea Whispers (1926). Jacobs published eighteen books in all during his lifetime; thirteen collections and five novels.

As a storyteller, Jacobs is perhaps better remembered for a handful of brief tales of the supernatural than for his popular nautical-themed works. The most famous of these, The Monkey's Paw, originally appeared as part of the 1902 short story collection The Lady of the Barge. It is an economically written story about a shriveled talisman, a monkey's paw that brings grief and horror in the wake of all too literal wish granting. The story has been adapted for other media repeatedly, starting with a one-act play performed at London's Haymarket Theatre in 1903. There have been multiple film adaptations of the story in the modern era; some of us are familiar with its appearance in an episode of the popular animated series, The Simpsons.

Another macabre gem, The Toll-House, was published as part of the collection Sailor's Knots in 1909. Jacob's once again employs a sparse style to tell the story of a group of men who spend the night in a famously haunted house on a dare (a noticeably similar narrative concept was put to use in the much earlier play The Ghost of Jerry Bundler, which had launched Jacobs' parallel career as a dramatist back in 1899 when it was produced at the St. James Theatre in London). Innovative at the time of writing, these sparingly written, atmospheric ghost stories are now familiar classics of the supernatural genre.

Though prolific in his younger years, Jacobs' productivity dropped dramatically after the start of World War I. Yet even in self-imposed semi-retirement Jacobs was still recognized as a leading humorist, ranked alongside such writers as P. G. Wodehouse and George Birmingham. He enjoyed continuing influence and elevated status among his fellow writers as evidenced by these comments attributed to his colleague Henry James:

"Mr. Jacobs, I envy you. You are popular! Your admirable work is appreciated by a wide circle of readers; it has achieved popularity. Mine never goes into a second edition."

James' literary fortunes would, of course, change, but his back-handedly complimentary admiration is compelling evidence of Jacobs' reputation as a writer and humourist both for his audience and his perhaps more admired literary colleagues.

Though Jacobs would create little in the way of new work after 1911, he was still writing. In these later years, seemingly burnt out creatively, Jacobs concentrated more on writing dramatizations and adaptations of his existing stories, including Beauty and the Barge (a film version starring Margaret Rutherford was also released in 1937) and In the Dark (a one act play that is often performed pr published with The Monkey's Paw adaptation).

Though admired by loyal readers throughout his lifetime, Jacobs has been almost completely forgotten since. Critics are at a loss to name a single reason why - Jacobs is universally considered to be a fine and imaginative literary craftsman. But, as critic John Wain suggested in a 1960 essay, perhaps Jacobs' humour may have been too gentle to persist into the cruel and sarcastic modern era, his dry pokes at proletariat hardship no longer suiting the times.

Nonetheless, Jacobs' legacy remains solid: he continued Dickens' (a writer with whom he is also often compared) tradition for sharing working class stories in authentic vernacular. And polished narratives such as The Monkey's Paw set a standard for the clever use of horror in fiction and popular culture that endures to this day. Indeed recently his works have begun to show an increased demand and appreciation in a world that is constantly looking over its shoulder.

William Wymark Jacobs died in a North London nursing home in Hornsey Lane, Islington on September 1st, 1943, just a week before his 80th birthday.

W.W. Jacobs – A Concise Bibliography

NOVELS AND SHORT STORY COLLECTIONS
MANY CARGOES (SHORT STORIES) (1896)
THE SKIPPER'S WOOING (1897)
SEA URCHINS (SHORT STORIES) (1898) aka MORE CARGOES
A MASTER OF CRAFT (1900)
LIGHT FREIGHTS (SHORT STORIES) (1901)
THE LADY OF THE BARGE (SHORT STORIES) (1902)
AT SUNWICH PORT (1902)
DIALSTONE LANE (1902)
SALTHAVEN (1908)
CAPTAINS ALL (SHORT STORIES) (1911)
NIGHT WATCHERS (SHORT STORIES) (1914)

DEEP WATERS (SHORT STORIES) (1919)

MRS. BUNKER'S CHAPERON
THE NEST EGG
ODD MAN OUT
THE OLD MAN OF THE SEA
OUTSAILED
OVER THE SIDE
PAYING OFF
THE PERSECUTION OF BOB PRETTY
PETER'S PENCE
PICKLED HERRING
PRIVATE CLOTHES
PRIZE MONEY
THE RESURRECTION OF MR. WIGGETT
THE RIVAL BEAUTIES
RULE OF THREE
SAM'S BOY
SAM'S GHOST
SELF-HELP
SENTENCE DEFERRED
SHAREHOLDERS
SKILLED ASSISTANCE
THE SKIPPER OF THE "OSPREY"
SMOKED SKIPPER
STEPPING BACKWARDS
STRIKING HARD
THE SUBSTITUTE
THE TEMPTATION OF SAMUEL BURGE
THE TEST
THE THREE SISTERS
TO HAVE AND TO HOLD
"THE TOLL-HOUSE"
TWIN SPIRITS
TWO OF A TRADE
THE UNDERSTUDY
THE UNKNOWN
THE VIGIL
WATCH-DOGS
THE WEAKER VESSEL
THE WELL
THE WHITE CAT

STAGE
THE GHOST OF JERRY BUNDLER (1899) (In London)

FILM ADAPTATIONS
A MASTER OF CRAFT (1922)
THE MONKEY'S PAW (1933)
OUR RELATIONS, a Laurel & Hardy film, "suggested by" to Jacobs' "The Money Box." (1936)
FOOTSTEPS IN THE FOG, from the short story The Interruption. (1955)